Enid Blyton

THE SECOND FORM AT ST CLARE'S

EGMONT

First published in Great Britain in 1941
by Methuen & Co. Ltd.

Copyright © Enid Blyton Limited 1941

Enid Blyton is a registered trademark of Enid Blyton Limited.

This edition distributed in 2005 by EuroKids International Private Ltd.
By arrangement with Egmont Books Limited, 239 Kensington High
Street, London, W8 6SA.

Printed in India.

A CIP catalogue record for this book
is available from the British Library.

CONTENTS

Enid Blyton

THE SECOND FORM
AT ST CLARE'S

Also by Enid Blyton

1 OFF TO SCHOOL AGAIN

THE last week of the summer holidays flew by, and the twins, Pat and Isabel O'Sullivan, seemed to be in a rush of buying clothes, fitting them on, looking out lacrosse sticks, finding lacrosse boots, and hunting for all kinds of things that seemed to have completely disappeared.

'Where is my knitting-bag?' said Pat, turning a whole drawer-full of things upside down. 'I know I brought it home at the end of last term.'

'I can only find *one* of my lacrosse boots,' wailed Isabel. 'Mummy, have you seen the other?'

'Yes, it came back from the bootmaker's yesterday,' said Mrs. O'Sullivan. 'Where did you put it?'

'Packing to go to school is always much more muddling than packing to come back home,' said Pat. 'I say, Isabel—won't it be fun to be in the second form this term?'

'Who is your form-teacher there?' asked their mother, unpacking half Pat's things and packing them all over again.

'Miss Jenks,' said Pat. 'I'll be sorry to leave Miss Roberts and the first form, in some ways. We did have fun there.'

'I bet we'll have some fun in Miss Jenks's class too,' said Isabel. 'I don't think she's quite so strict as Miss Roberts.'

'Don't you believe it!' said Isabel, trying to cram a tin of toffees into a corner. 'She may not have Miss Roberts's sarcastic tongue-but she's all there! Don't you remember how she used to deal with Tessie when Tessie used to try on her pretend-sneezes?'

'Yes—sent her to Matron for a large dose of awful medicine, supposed to stop a cold!' giggled Pat. 'All the same, I bet we'll get away with quite a lot of things in Miss Jenks's form.'

'I hope you mean to work,' said Mrs. O'Sullivan, putting in the top tray of Isabel's trunk. 'I was quite pleased with last term's report. Don't let me have a bad one as soon as you go up into another form, will you?'

'We'll work all right, Mummy,' said Pat. 'I can tell you, the teachers at St. Clare's aren't easy-going where work is concerned. They keep our noses to the grindstone! Mam'zelle's the worst. She really seems to think we ought to learn to talk French better than we speak English!'

'No wonder your French accent is so much improved, then,' said Mrs. O'Sullivan, with a laugh. 'Now Pat—let me see if I can possibly shut your trunk. You'd better sit on it whilst I try to shut the clasps.'

The trunk wouldn't shut. Mrs. O'Sullivan opened it again and looked inside. 'You can't take all those books,' she said, firmly.

'Mummy, I *must*,' said Pat. 'And I simply must take those games too—we love jigsaws in the winter term.'

'Well, Pat, all I can say is, you'd better take books, games, toffees, biscuits and knitting things, and leave behind your clothes,' said the twins' mother. 'Now—be sensible—take out three books and we can shut the trunk,'

Pat took out three books, and, when Mrs. O'Sullivan was not looking, put them hurriedly into Isabel's trunk. Her own trunk now shut down fairly easily, and was locked. Then Mrs. O'Sullivan went to Isabel's.

'This won't shut, either,' she said. 'Gracious, the things you girls take back with you to boarding-school nowadays! When I...'

'When *you* were a girl you only took a small case, and that held everything!' chanted the twins, who had heard these remarks before. 'Mummy, we'll *both* sit on Isabel's trunk, shall we?'

Mrs. O'Sullivan opened the trunk and firmly removed three books from the top layer. She looked at them in surprise. 'I seem to have seen these before!' she said. The twins giggled. They sat on the trunk and it shut with a groan.

'And now to pack your hand-bag with night-things in,' said Mrs. O'Sullivan, looking at the school-list to make sure nothing had been forgotten. 'That won't take long.'

Night-gowns, tooth-brushes, face-flannels and sponges went into small bags. Then the twins were ready. They were both dressed neatly in their school winter uniforms of grey, with blue blouses and scarlet ties. They put on grey coats and grey felt hats with the school ribbon round, and looked at each other.

'Two good little St. Clare girls,' said Pat, looking demure.

'Not so very good,' said her mother, with a smile 'Now-there is the car at the door, ready to take us to the station. Have we really got everything? You must write and tell me if you want anything else.'

'Oh, we're sure to want lots of things!' said Pat. 'You're a darling, the way you send us things. It's fun to be going back to St. Clare's. I'm awfully glad you sent us there, Mummy.'

'And how you hated going at first!' said Mrs. O'Sullivan, remembering the fuss the twins had made, because they had wanted to go to another, much more expensive school.

'Yes—we made up our minds to be so awful that the school wouldn't keep us,' said Pat. 'And we *were* awful too—but we couldn't keep it up. St. Clare's was too much for us—we just *had* to be decent in the end!'

'Do come on,' said Isabel. 'We shall miss the train! I'm longing to meet all the girls in London, and see them again, aren't you, Pat? I do like the journey down to St. Clare's.'

They were off at last. They had to travel to London, and go to the station where the St. Clare train started. The whole train was reserved for the St. Clare girls, for it was a big school.

There was a terrific noise on the platform, where scores of girls were waiting for the train. Their mothers were there to bid them good-bye, and teachers moved about, trying to collect the girls together. Porters shoved luggage into the van, and everyone was excited.

'Bobby! Oh, there's Bobby!' yelled Pat, as soon as they arrived on the crowded platform. 'And Janet too. Hie Bobby, hie, Janet!'

'Hallo, twins!' cried Bobby. Her merry eyes crinkled up as she smiled.

'It's good to see your turn-up nose again,' said Pat, slipping her arm through Bobby's. 'Hallo, Janet! Got any more tricks from that brother of yours?'

'Wait and see,' grinned Janet. A mistress came up at that moment and overheard the remarks.

'Ah-did I hear the word TRICKS, Janet?' she said. 'Well, just remember you're in *my* form this term, and there are really Terrible Punishments for tricks like yours!'

'Yes, Miss Jenks,' grinned Janet. 'I'll remember. Are all the others here yet?'

'All but Doris,' said Miss Jenks. 'Ah, there she is. Now we must get into the train. The guard is looking rather worried, I see.'

'Carlotta! Get into our carriage!' yelled Bobby, seeing the dark-eyed, dark-haired girl running down the platform. 'What sort of hols, did you have? Did you go back to the circus?'

Carlotta was a source of great attraction and admiration to the girls, for she had once been a circus-girl, and her understanding and handling of horses was marvellous. Now she had to settle down at St. Clare's, and learn many things she had never heard of. She had found her first term very difficult, but at the end of it she was firm friends with most of her form, and the mistresses were pleased with her. She ran up to the twins and Bobby, her vivid little face glowing with pleasure.

'Hallo!' she said, 'I'll get into your carriage. Oh, look —there's your cousin Alison. She looks rather miserable.'

'I *feel* miserable,' said Alison O'Sullivan, coming up, looking very woe-begone. 'I shall miss my friend Sadie dreadfully this term.'

Sadie had been an American girl with no ideas in her head at all beyond clothes and the cinema. She had had a very bad influence on Alison, but as she was not coming back that term, it was to be hoped that the feather-headed Alison would pull herself together a little, and try to do better. She was a pretty little thing who easily burst into tears. Her cousins welcomed her warmly.

'Hallo, Alison! Don't fret about Sadie. You'll soon find other friends.'

They all got into the carriage. Doris arrived, panting. Hilary Wentworth, who had been head of the first form, flung herself down in a corner seat. She was very much wondering if she would be head of the second form. She was a trustworthy and responsible girl who liked being head.

'Hallo, everybody,' she said. 'Nice to see you all again. Well, Carlotta—been riding in the Ring, I suppose! Lucky kid!'

'You know I don't belong to a circus any more,' said Carlotta. 'I went to spend my holidays with my father and my grandmother. My father seems to like me quite a lot-but my grandmother found a lot of fault with my manners. She says I must pay more attention to them this term even than to my lessons! You must all help me!'

'Oh no!' said Pat, with a laugh. 'We don't want you any different from what you are, my dear, hot-tempered, entirely natural, perfectly honest little Carlotta! We get more fun out of you than out of anyone. We don't want you changed one little bit! Any more than we want Bobby changed. We shall expect some marvellous tricks from you this term, Bobby.'

'Right,' said Bobby. 'But I tell you here and now, I'm going to work too!'

'Miss Jenks will see to that,' said Hilary. 'Remember we shall no longer be in the bottom form. We've got to work for exams, and pass them!'

'We're off!' said Pat, leaning out of the window. 'Good-bye, Mummy! We'll write on Sunday!'

The train steamed slowly out of the station. The girls drew in their heads. All the carriages were full of chatterers, talking about the wonderful hols. they had had, the places they had been to, and what sort of term it would be.

'Any new girls?' said Isabel. 'I haven't seen one.'

'I think there's only one,' said Bobby. 'We saw a miserable-looking creature standing a little way up the platform —I don't know whether she'll be second form or first form. Not second, I hope—she looked such a misery!'

'Alison's doing her hair again already,' said Pat. 'Alison!

Put your comb away. Girls, I think we'll have to make it a rule that Alison doesn't do her hair more than fifty times a day!'

Every one laughed. It was good to be back, good to be all together once more. The winter term was going to be fun!

2 IN THE SECOND FORM

IT was very strange at first to be in the second form, instead of the first. The twins felt very important, and looked down on the first-formers, feeling that they were very young and unimportant. But the third-formers also looked down on the second form, so things soon shook themselves out, and every one settled down.

'It's funny to go to the second form class-room instead of to Miss Roberts's room,' said Pat. 'I keep on going to the first form room, as I always used to do.'

'So do I,' said Janet. 'Miss Roberts is beginning to think we're doing it on purpose. We'd better be careful.'

'There's a whole lot of new girls in the first form, after all,' said Pat. 'Miss Roberts must have collected them altogether on the train. That's why we didn't see them. There's about twelve!'

'I shall never know all their names,' said Isabel. 'Any-way—they're only little kids—some of them not yet fourteen!'

'All the first-formers have been moved up,' said Bobby. 'Except young Pam—and she's only just fourteen. I bet she'll be head of the first form!'

Pam Boardman had been new the term before, and was a very hard-working child. As Bobby said, she was made head of the first form, and was extremely proud of the honour. She had many new girls under her, and was eager to help them all.

Only two girls had been left down in the second form-Elsie Fanshawe and Anna Johnson. The girls who had just come up were sorry to see them there, for they were not much liked. Elsie Fanshawe was spiteful, and Anna Johnson was lazy.

'I suppose one of them will be head girl,' said Hilary, with a grimace. 'Well—I don't fancy either of them, do you, Bobby?'

'They both think themselves very superior to us,' said Bobby. 'Just because they've been second-formers for a year.'

'I should be ashamed,' said Carlotta. 'I would not like to spend more than a year in any form. But Anna is so lazy she will never get up into the third form, I'm sure!'

'I believe Miss Jenks didn't send them up because she hoped they'd buck up a bit if they were heads,' said Pat. 'I rather think she's going to make them joint head girls. We shall have to look out if Elsie's head-she's really catty.'

'We've got that Misery-girl in our form after all,' said Bobby, looking at the new girl, who was standing mournfully not far off, looking at nothing. 'She never says a word, but looks as if she'll burst into tears at any moment!'

The Misery-girl, as the others called her, was named Gladys Hillman. The girls tried to make her talk and Bobbie did her best to make her laugh, but Gladys took no notice of any one. She walked by herself, seemed to dream all the time, and hardly spoke a word.

'Better leave her alone,' said Hilary. 'Perhaps she's homesick.'

Not many of the St. Clare girls felt home-sick when they returned to school, because it was all so jolly and friendly, and there was so much to do that there seemed no time to miss home and parents. The beginning of term was always fun—new books given out, new girls to size up, new desks to sit in, and sometimes new forms to go to.

'There's a new mistress,' said Bobby, in excitement. 'She's to take Elocution and Drama! Look—there she is-isn't she dark?'

Miss Quentin certainly was dark, and extremely good looking. She had black piercing eyes, and a beautiful voice. Alison thought she was wonderful.

'You *would*!' said Bobby. 'You'll be doing your hair like Miss Quentin next, swept over your brow and round your ears. There'll always be some one for you to copy, my dear Alison! Do you remember last term how you copied everything your dear friend Sadie did?'

Alison flushed. She was always being teased and she never seemed to get used to it. She turned away with a toss of her pretty head. The others laughed at her. There was nothing bad in Alison—but on the other hand there was nothing very good either. She was, as Pat so often said, 'just a pretty little feather-head!'

The second form soon settled down with Miss Jenks. At first it seemed strange to them not to have Miss Roberts teaching them for most of the morning. They missed her dry remarks and crisp words of praise. Miss Jenks was not so shrewd as Miss Roberts, nor was she so cool when angry. She could not bear the slightest hint of rudeness, and she had no sympathy at all for 'frills and fancies' as she put it. No girl dared to fuss her hair out too much, or to wear anything but a plain gold bar for a brooch in Miss Jenks's class.

'Alison is in for a bad time!' grinned Bobby one morning, when Alison had been sent to remove a bow from her hair and a brooch from her collar.

'So is Carlotta!' said Pat. 'Miss Jenks doesn't like frills and fancies—but she doesn't like untidiness either! Just *look* at your hair, Carlotta. It's wild enough in the ordinary way-but it looks like a golliwog's hair at the moment.'

'Does it really?' said Carlotta, who never cared in the least what she looked like. 'Well, those sums we had to do were so hard I just had to clutch my hair all the time!'

'Old Mam'zelle's still the same,' said Isabel. 'Funny, old, hot-tempered, flat-footed thing—but I like her all the same. She always gives us *some* excitement—and I bet she will this term, too. Do you remember how she and Carlotta nearly came to blows last term?'

Yes—the summer term had been a very exciting one. The girls looked at Mam'zelle and remembered all the jokes they had played on her. Dear old Mam'zelle, she always fell for everything. She was very terrifying when she lost her temper, but she had a great sense of humour, and when her short-sighted eyes twinkled behind their glasses, the girls felt a real fondness for her.

'Ah,' said Mam'zelle, looking round the second form. 'Ah! You are now the second form—very important, very responsible, and very hard-working, *n'est pas*? The first-formers, they are babies, they know nothing-but as soon as you arrive in the second form, you are big girls, you know a great deal!. Your French will be quite per-r-r-rfect! And Doris-ah, even Doris will be able to roll her R's in the proper French way!'

Every one laughed. Poor Doris, always bottom at oral French, could never roll her R's. Doris grinned. She was a dunce, but nobody minded. She was a wonderful mimic and could keep the whole form in roars of laughter when she liked.

'R-r-r-r-r-r-!' said Carlotta, unexpectedly. She sounded like an aeroplane taking off, and Mam'zelle frowned.

'You are now in the second form, Carlotta,' she said, coldly. 'We do not do those things here.'

'No, Mam'zelle,' said Carlotta, meekly. 'Of course not.'

'Tricks and jokes are not performed in any form higher than the first,' warned Mam'zelle. 'Whilst you are first-form babies, one does not expect much from you-but as soon as you leave the bottom form behind, it is different. We expect you to behave with dignity. One day the head-girl may be one of you here, and it is not too soon to pre-pare for such an honour.'

Winifred James, the much-admired head-girl, had left, and Belinda Towers, the sports captain, had taken her place. This was a very popular choice, for Belinda was well known by the whole school, and very much liked. As a sports captain she knew practically all the girls, and this would be a great help to her as head-girl. She was not so gentle and quiet as Winifred, and many girls were afraid of her out-spokenness, but there was no doubt she would make an excellent head-girl.

Belinda visited every common room in turn and made the same short speech to the girls there.

'You all know I'm head-girl now—and I'm still sports-captain too. You can come to me if you're in a spot of trouble at any time and I'll help if I can. You'll all have to toe the mark where games are concerned, because I want to put St. Clare's right on the map this winter, with lacrosse. We must win every match we play!

'We've got some fine players for a school team, but I want every form to supply players for the second and third match-teams too. So buck up, all of you, and prac-tise hard.'

Alison groaned as Belinda went out of the second form common room. 'Why *do* we have to play games?' she said. 'They just make us hot and untidy and tired.'

'You forget they do other things as well,' said Janet. 'We have to learn to work together as a team—each one for his side, helping the others, not each one for himself. That sort of thing is especially good for *you*, my dear Alison —you'd sit in a corner and look at yourself in the mirror all day long if you could—and a fat lot of good that would do to you or anybody else.'

'Oh, be quiet,' said Alison. 'You're always getting at me!'

It *was* fun to be back again, and to hear all the familiar school chatter, to groan over prep., to eat enormous teas, to talk about lacrosse, to laugh at somebody's joke, and to look forward to the class you liked the best—painting, maybe, or music, or elocution— or even maths!

There was a surprise for the second form at the end of the first week. Another new girl appeared! She arrived at tea-time, with red eyes and a sulky mouth. She looked defiantly at every one as she took her place at the second form table.

'This is Mirabel Unwin,' said Miss Jenks. 'She has arrived rather late for beginning of term—but still, better late than never, Mirabel.'

'I didn't want to come at all,' said Mirabel, in a loud voice. 'They tried to make me come on the right day but I wouldn't. I only came now because my father promised I could leave at half-term if I'd come now. I suppose he thought once he got me here I'd stay. But I shan't.'

'That will do, Mirabel,' said Miss Jenks, soothingly. 'You are tired and over-wrought. Don't say any more. You will soon settle down and be happy.'

'No, I shan't,' said the surprising Mirabel. 'I shan't settle down and I shan't be happy. I shan't try at anything, because what's the use if I'm leaving at half-term?'

'Well, we'll see,' said Miss Jenks. 'Be sensible now and eat some tea. You must be hungry.'

The girls stared at Mirabel. They were not used to people who shouted their private affairs out in public. They thought Mirabel was rather shocking-but rather exciting too.

'I thought she was another Misery-girl at first, but I believe she's just spoilt and peevish,' said Pat. 'I say-the second form is going to be quite an exciting place this term!'

3   TWO HEAD-GIRLS AND TWO NEW GIRLS

MISS JENKS made both the old second-formers into joint head-girls of the form. She and Miss Theobald, the Head Mistress, had had a talk about them, and had decided that perhaps it would be the making of them.

'Elsie is a spiteful type,' said Miss Jenks. 'She has never been popular, though she would have liked to be— so she gets back at the others by being spiteful and saying nasty things. And Anna is bone-lazy—won't do a thing if she can help it!'

'Well, a little responsibility may be good for them,' said Miss Theobald, thoughtfully. 'It will give Elsie a sense of importance, and bring out any good in her—and Anna will have to bestir herself if she wants to keep her position. Let them both try.'

'I don't know how they will work together,' said Miss Jenks, doubtfully. 'They don't like each other very much.'

'Let them try,' said Miss Theobald. 'Elsie is quick, and she may stir Anna up a bit—and Anna is too lazy to be spiteful, so perhaps she will be good for Elsie in that way. But I too have my doubts!'

Elsie Fanshawe was delighted to be a joint head-girl—though, of course, she would very much rather have been the only one. Still, after being thoroughly disliked and kept down by the whole of the second form, it was quite a change to be top-dog!

'Now I can jolly well keep the others down and make them look up to *me*,' thought Elsie, pleased. 'I can get some of my own back. These silly little first-formers, who have just come up, have got to learn to knuckle under a bit. I can make Anna agree with all I do—lazy thing! I'll have every single one of the rules kept, and, and I'll make a few of my own, if I want to—and I'll report any one who gets out of hand. It's worth-while not going up into the third form, to be top of the second!'

The others guessed a little what Elsie was thinking. Although they had not known the girl very well when they were first-formers, they had heard the others talking about her. They knew Elsie would try to 'get her own back.'

'Just what a head-girl shouldn't do,' said Janet. 'She should try and set some sort of example to the others, or what's the use of being a leader? Look at old Hilary, when she was head of the first form! She was a good sport and joined in everything—but she always knew where to draw the line without getting our backs up.'

'I can't bear Elsie,' said Carlotta. 'I would like to slap her hard.'

'Oh Carlotta! Have you still got that habit?' said Bobby, pretending to be shocked. 'Really, a second-former, too! What *would* Elsie say!'

Elsie overheard the last remark. 'What would I say to what?' she asked, coming up.

'Oh, nothing—Carlotta was simply saying she'd like to slap some one,' said Bobby, with a grin.

'Please understand, Carlotta, that you are in the second form now,' said Elsie, in a cold voice. 'We don't even *talk* of slapping people!'

'Yes, we do,' said Carlotta. 'Wouldn't you like to know whom I want to slap, dear Elsie?'

Elsie heard the danger note in Carlotta's high voice, and put her nose in the air.

'I'm not interested in your slapping habits,' she said and walked off.

'Shut up now, Carlotta,' said Bobby. 'Don't go and get all wild and Spanish again. You were bad enough with Prudence last term!'

'Well, thank goodness old Sour-Milk Prudence was expelled!' said Carlotta. 'I wouldn't have stayed if she had come back!'

It was the hour when all the second form were in their common room, playing, working or chattering. They loved being together like that. The wireless blared at one end of the room, and Doris and Bobby danced a ridiculous dance to the music. Gladys Hillman sat in a corner, looking as miserable as usual. Nobody could make anything of her. Isabel looked at her and felt sorry. She went over to her.

'Come and dance,' she said. Gladys shook her head. 'What's the matter?' asked Isabel. 'Are you home-sick? You'll soon get over it.'

'Don't bother me,' said Gladys. 'I don't bother you.'

'Yes, you do,' said Isabel. 'You bother me a lot. I can't bear to see you sitting here all alone, looking so miserable. Haven't you been to boarding-school before?

'No,' said Gladys. Her eyes filled with tears. Isabel felt a little impatient with her. Hadn't she any courage at all?

'You don't seem to enjoy a single thing,' said Isabel. 'Don't you like any lesson specially—or games—or something?'

'I like acting,' said Gladys, unexpectedly. 'And I like lacrosse. That's all. But I don't like them here. I don't like anything here.'

She wouldn't say any more, and Isabel gave her up. She went across to Pat. 'Hopeless!' she said. 'Just a mass of self-pity and tears! She'll fade away and we'll never notice she's gone if she doesn't buck up! I'd almost rather have that rude Mirabel than Gladys.'

Mirabel had been the source of much annoyance and amusement to the second form. She was rude to the point of being unbearable, and reminded every one every day that she wasn't going to stay a day beyond halfterm.

'Don't tell me that any more,' begged Bobby. 'You can't imagine how glad I am you're going at half-term. It's the only bright spot I can see. But I warn you—don't be too rude to Mam'zelle, or sparks will fly—and don't get on the high horse too much with our dear head-girl, Elsie Fanshawe, or you'll get the worst of it. Elsie is pretty clever you know, and you're rather stupid.'

'No, I'm not!' flashed Mirabel, angrily. 'I only seem stupid because I don't want to try—but you should hear me play the piano and the violin! *Then* you'd see!'

'Why, you don't even *learn* music!' said Bobby. 'And I've never seen you open your mouth in the singing class. We all came to the conclusion that you couldn't sing a note.'

'That's all *you* know!' said Mirabel, rudely. 'Golly, what a school this is! I always knew boarding-school would be awful—but it's worse that I expected. I hate living with a lot of rude girls who think they're the cat's whiskers just because they've been here a year or two!'

'Oh, you make me tired,' said Bobby, and walked off. 'Really, what with you and the Misery-girl, and spiteful old Elsie we're badly off this term!'

Miss Jenks kept a very firm hand on Mirabel. 'You may not intend to work,' she said, 'but you are not going to stop the others from working! You will do one of three things, my dear Mirabel—you will stay in the classroom and work—or you will stay in the classroom and do nothing at all, not even say a word—or you will go and stand *out*side the classroom till the lesson is finished!'

At first Mirabel thought it was marvellous to defy Miss Jenks and be sent outside. But she soon found it wearisome to stand there so long, waiting for the others to come out. Also, she was always a little afraid that the Head Mistress, Miss Theobald, would come along. Loudly as Mirabel declared that she cared for nobody, nobody at all at silly St. Clare's, she *was* in awe of the quiet Head Mistress.

'Did you tell Miss Theobald that you didn't mean to stay here longer than half-term?' asked Pat. Every girl had to go to see the Head Mistress when she arrived on the first day.

'Of course I did!' said Mirabel, tossing her head. 'I told her *I* didn't care for anyone, not even the Head!'

This was untrue. Mirabel had meant to say quite a lot —but Miss Theobald had somehow said it first. She had looked gravely at the red-eyed girl when she had come in and had told her to sit down. Mirabel opened her mouth to speak, but Miss Theobald silenced her.

'I must finish this letter,' she said. 'Then we will talk.'
She kept Mirabel waiting for ten minutes. The girl studied
the Head's calm face, and felt a little awed. It would be
difficult to be rude to someone like this. The longer she
waited, the more difficult it would be to say what she had
meant to say.

Miss Theobald raised her head at last. 'Well,
Mirabel,' she said, 'I know you feel upset, angry and
defiant. Your father insisted you should come away to
school because you are spoilt and make his home unbearable. You also domineer over your smaller brother
and sister. He chose St. Clare's because he thought we
might be able to do something for you. No—don't interrupt me. Believe me, I know all you want to say—but you
don't know what *I* have to say.'

There was a pause. Even defiant Mirabel did not
dare to say a word.

'We have had many difficult girls here,' said Miss
Theobald. 'We rather pride ourselves on getting the
best out of them. You see, Mirabel, difficult children
often have fine things hidden in their characters—things that
perhaps more ordinary children don't possess....'

'What things?' asked Mirabel, interested in spite of herself.

'Well—sometimes difficult children have a great talent
for something—a gift for art or drama, a talent for music-or
maybe they have some great quality—out standing courage, perhaps. Well, I don't know if this is the case with
you, or whether you are just a spoilt and unruly girl—we
shall see. All I want to say now is—give yourself a chance
and let me see if there is anything worth—while in you this
half-term. If there is not, we don't want you to stay. We
shall be glad for you to go.'

This was so unexpected that Mirabel again had nothing

to say. She had meant to say that nothing on earth would make her stay at St. Clare's beyond the half-term—but here was Miss Theobald saying that she didn't want to keep her longer than that—unless—unless she was worth-while! Worth-while!

'I don't care if I'm worth-while or not!' thought Mirabel to herself, indignantly. 'And how dare Daddy write and tell Miss Theobald those things about me? Why couldn't he keep our affairs to himself?'

Mirabel voiced this thought aloud. 'I think it was horrid of my father to tell you things about me,' she said, in a trembling voice.

'They were said in confidence to some one who understood," said Miss Theobald. 'Have you kept your own tongue quiet about *your* private affairs this afternoon, Mirabel? No—I rather think you gave yourself away to the whole school at tea-time when you arrived!'

Mirabel flushed. Yes—she could not keep control over her tongue.

'You may go,' said Miss Theobald, picking up her pen again. 'And remember—it is not *St. Clare's* which is on trial—it is *you*! I hope I shall not say good-bye to you and rejoice to see the last of you at half-term. But—I shall not be surprised if I do!'

Mirabel went out of the room, her ears tingling, her face still red. She had been used to getting all her own way, to letting her rough tongue say what it pleased, and to ruling her parents and brother and sister as she pleased. When her father had at last declared in anger that she must go away, there had been a royal battle between them. The spoilt girl had imagined she could rule the roost at St. Clare's too. But she certainly could not rule Miss Theobald!

'Never mind—I'll lead everyone else a dance!' she thought. 'I'll show Daddy and the others that I mean what

I say! I won't be sent away from home if I don't want to go.'

And so Mirabel set herself to be as annoying as possible, to spoil things for the others, and to try and domineer in the classroom, as she had always done at home. But she had not bargained for the treatment she got at last from an exasperated class.

4   MIRABEL IS A NUISANCE

THE second form did not so much mind when Mirabel was annoying in classes they disliked, such as the maths. class, which they found difficult that term—or even in Mam'zelle's class when she took irregular French verbs, hated by every girl. But they did dislike it when she spoilt, or tried to spoil, the English class, or the Art class.

'It spoils our reading of *The Tempest*, when you make idiotic remarks, or flop about in your seat and make Miss Jenks keep on saying "Sit up!" ' said Hilary, angrily. 'Either behave badly enough to get sent out of the room at once, idiot, or else keep quiet.'

'And if you dare to upset your paint-water all over somebody again, and make us lose ten minutes of the art class whilst we all get ticked off by Miss Walker I'll scrag you,' said Carlotta, all in one breath. 'We wouldn't mind so much if you did something really funny, like Bobby or Janet did last term—what you do *isn't* funny-just idiotic, spoiling things for the whole class.'

'I shall do what I like,' said Mirabel.

'You will not,' said Elsie, spitefully. 'I'm head-girl of this form—with Anna—and we say you are to behave yourself, or we'll know the reason why.'

'You do know the reason why,' said Mirabel, pertly.

'Any one would think you were six years old, the way you behave,' said Bobby, in disgust. 'Well—I warn you—you'll be sorry if you keep on like this. We're all getting tired of you.'

The explosion came during the Drama class. This was taken by the new teacher, Miss Quentin, and was really rather an exciting class. The girls were to write and act their own play. Dark-eyed Miss Quentin was full of good suggestions, and the play was almost written.

The new teacher was not much good at discipline. She relied on her good looks and rather charming manner, and on the interest of her lessons, to help her to discipline her classes. Alison adored her, and, as the girls had already foreseen, was copying her in everything, from her little tricks of speech, to the way she did her hair.

Most of the girls liked Miss Quentin, though they did not very much respect the way she coaxed them to behave when they became a little unruly. They really preferred the downright methods of Miss Roberts or Miss Jenks. Mirabel, of course, soon found that Miss Quentin was quite unable to keep her in order.

'Your turn now, Mirabel dear,' Miss Quentin would say, smiling brightly at her. Mirabel would pretend not to hear, and Miss Quentin would raise her voice slightly.

'Mirabel! Your turn now, dear!'

The class disliked Miss Quentin's 'dears' and 'lambs' and other names—except Alison. She loved them. They all looked at Mirabel impatiently. She was always losing time like this, when they wanted to get on.

Mirabel would pretend to come back to earth with a start, fumble for the place, be gently helped by Miss Quentin, and at last say something, usually incorrect. When there was any acting to be done she came in at the wrong moment, said the wrong lines, and altogether behaved in a most annoying manner. Miss Quentin was at a loss to know how to deal with her.

'Mirabel! I have never yet sent a girl out of my class,' she would say, in such a sorrowful voice that it quite wrung Alison's heart. 'Now come-pull yourself together and try again.'

One morning Alison was waiting to act a part she loved. She had rehearsed it over and over again to herself, acting it, as she thought, to perfection. She was longing for her turn to come, so that she might gloat over the sugared words of praise she felt sure would drop from Miss Quentin's lips.

There were ten more minutes to go—just about time for Alison's turn to come. And then Mirabel chose to be stupid again, saying her lines incorrectly, doing the wrong things so that Miss Quentin had to make her speak and act two or three times. The teacher, following her usual rule of being patient and encouraging, wasted nearly all the precious ten minutes on Mirabel.

Alison cast her eye on the clock, and bit her lip. All her rehearsing would be wasted now. How she hated that stupid Mirabel, holding up every class in order to be annoying.

'Now Mirabel *dear*,' psaid Miss Quentin, in her charming, patient voice, 'say it like this...'

It was too much for Alison. She stamped her foot. 'Mirabel! Stop fooling! It's hateful the way you take Miss Quentin in—and she's so patient too. You've wasted half the time—and now I shan't have my turn.'

'Poor little Alison!' said Mirabel, mockingly. 'She so badly wanted to show off to her precious Miss Quentin, and hear her say "Well done, *darling*!"'

There was a dead silence. Then Alison burst into a flood of tears, and Carlotta boxed Mirabel's ears very neatly and smartly. Miss Quentin stared in horror.

'Girls! Girls! What are you thinking of? Carlotta! You amaze me. I cannot have this behaviour, I really cannot. Carlotta, apologize at once to Mirabel.'

'Certainly not,' said Carlotta. 'I don't mean to be rude to *you*, Miss Quentin—but you must see for yourself that Mirabel deserved it. I knew no one else but me would dare to do it—and it's been coming to Mirabel for quite a long time.'

The bell rang for the next class. Miss Quentin was most relieved. She had no idea how to tackle things of this sort. She gathered up her books quickly.

'There is no time to say any more, girls,' she said. 'I must go to my next class. Carlotta, I still insist that you put things right with Mirabel by apologizing.'

She went out of the room in a flurry. Carlotta grinned round at the others. 'Well!' she said, 'don't stand staring at me like that as if I'd done something awful. You know quite well you've all wanted to box Mirabel's ears yourselves. We're as tired of her as we can be. It's a pity half-term isn't here and we can see the back of her.'

'Carlotta, you shouldn't do things like that,' said Janet. 'Alison, for pity's sake, stop howling. Mirabel, you deserved it, and now perhaps you'll shut up and behave properly.'

Mirabel had gone rather white. She had not attempted to hit back at Carlotta. 'If you think that will stop me doing what I like to spoil things for anybody you're mistaken,' she said, at last, in a tight kind of voice. 'It'll make me worse.'

'I suppose it will,' said Hilary. 'Well—I'll give you a warning. If you don't stop being an idiot, *we* shall make things uncomfortable for *you*. I don't mean we shall box your ears. We shan't. But there are other ways.'

Mirabel said no more—but as she made no attempt that day or the following to behave sensibly, the girls made up their minds that they must carry out their threat.

They met in one of the music-rooms. Elsie Fanshawe was pleased. This excited her—it gladdened her spiteful nature, and added to her sense of importance for, as she was one of the head-girls, she could direct every one in what they had to do.

'We've met together to decide how to get back at Mirabel,' she began.

Hilary interrupted her. 'Well—not exactly "get back," Elsie,' she said. 'It's more to prevent her from going on disgracing herself and our class.'

'Call it what you like,' said Elsie, impatiently. 'Now-what I propose is this: we'll take her books from her desk and hide them. We'll make her an apple-pie bed each night. We'll stitch up the pockets and sleeves of her out-door coat. We'll put stones into her Wellingtons. We'll...'

'It all sounds rather spiteful,' said Hilary, doubtfully. 'Need we do quite so many things? I know Mirabel is perfectly sickening and needs a good lesson—but don't let's make ourselves as bad as she is!'

'Well—do as you like,' said Elsie, rather sneeringly. 'If you're too goody-goody to follow the lead of your head-girls, well, there will be plenty of us who'll do what I say.'

'I bet Anna didn't think of any of those things,' said Bobby, looking at the plump, placid Anna, sitting beside Elsie.

The meeting discussed the matter a little more, and then, at the sound of a school-bell, broke up. Only Gladys had said nothing. She had sat, as usual, in a kind of dream, paying hardly any attention to what was said. The

Carlotta boxed Mirabel's ears very smartly

girls were becoming so used to the Misery-girl, as they called her, that they really hardly noticed whether she was there or not.

'Well,' said Hilary, as the girls ran off to change for games, 'I suppose we must do something to teach Mirabel that two can play at being annoying—but somehow a lot of spitefulness seems to have got mixed up in it.'

'It's bound to, with Elsie Fanshawe to lead us !' said Bobby. 'I wish she wasn't our head-girl. She's not the right sort. As for Anna, she's no use at all—just a lazy lump!'

'Mirabel's going to have a few shocks from now on,' said Alison, who was more pleased than anyone to think of the tricks that were to be played on Mirabel. 'I for one will do everything with the greatest pleasure!'

'I hope your darling Miss Quentin will be pleased with you!' said Bobby, with a grin, and scampered off to the field before Alison could think of any reply.

5   MIRABEL AND THE
MISERY-GIRL

IT was not pleasant to be thought a tiresome nuisance by girls and teachers alike. Mirabel was getting tired of her defiant pose. Nobody had ever thought it was funny, as she had hoped. Nobody had ever laughed. They had just got impatient. The girl began to feel sorry she had ever started her irritating behaviour.

A great feeling of misery overtook her the evening

of the day she had been slapped by Carlotta. She felt that no one liked her, and certainly no one loved her. Hadn't her own father sent her away? And her mother had agreed to it! How could she put up with that? There was no way to answer things like that except by being defiant.

Mirabel felt that she did not want to be with the others that evening in the noisy common room. She stole away by herself to one of the music-rooms. She had spoken truly when she had told Bobby that she could play the piano and the violin. She loved music, and was a really good performer on the piano, and a beautiful player of the violin. But because of her defiant obstinacy, she had refused to learn either of the instruments at St. Clare's, when her father had spoken to her about them.

'You can learn well there,' he told her. 'There are excellent teachers of both.'

'What's the use!' Mirabel had flashed at him. 'I'm only going to be there for half a term—and you don't want to have to pay full fees for two lots of music lessons, do you, as well as full fees for the ordinary lesson?'

'Very well. Have it your own way,' said her father. So nothing had been said about learning music, and the girls had missed her weekly lessons very much. Music had always helped her strong, domineering nature—and now, without it, she felt lost. She was depressed and unhappy tonight—her mind longed for something to fasten on, something to love. She thought of her violin at home, and wished with all her heart that she had brought it with her.

It was dark in the music-room. Mirabel did not turn on the light, for she was afraid somebody passing might see her, and she did not want any company just then. She leaned her arms on a little table and thought.

Her hands touched something—a violin case. Something in the feel of it stirred her, and suddenly, with hands that trembled a little, she undid the strap and took out the violin inside. She put it lovingly under her chin, and groped for the bow.

And then the little dark music-room was full of music, as Mirabel played to herself. She played to comfort herself, to forget herself, and the notes filled the little room, and made it beautiful.

'That's better,' said Mirabel at last. 'That's much better! I didn't know how much I'd missed my music. I wonder whereabouts the piano is. I'll play that too. Why didn't I think of this before?'

She groped her way to the piano, and began to finger the notes gently in the darkness. She played from memory, and chose melodies that were sad and yearning, to match her own mood.

She thought she was alone, and she put her whole heart into her playing. Then suddenly she heard a sound in the room beside her, and she stopped at once, her heart thumping. She heard a stifled sob.

'Who's there?' said Mirabel, in a low voice. There was no answer. Someone began softly to grope her way to the door. Mirabel felt a stir of anger. Who was it spying on her? Who had come into the room like that? She jumped up and grabbed wildly at the some one near the door. She caught a blouse sleeve and held on.

'Who is it?' she said.

'Me—Gladys,' said a voice. 'I was in here alone—when you came in. I didn't know you were going to play. But you played such beautiful music I had to stay—and then it got sad, and I cried.'

'You're always crying,' said Mirabel, impatiently. 'What's the matter?'

'I shan't tell you,' said Gladys. 'You'll only tell the others, and they'd laugh. They call me Misery-girl, I know. It's hateful. They'd be Misery-girls too if they were like me.'

'Like *you*—why, what's the matter with you?' asked

Mirabel, her curiosity aroused. 'Look here—tell me. I shan't jeer at you or anything.'

'Well, don't turn on the light then,' said Gladys. 'You'll think I'm very feeble, so I'd rather tell you in the dark.'

'You *are* a queer fish,' said Mirabel. 'Come on-what's the matter?'

'It's my mother,' said Gladys. 'She's awfully ill—in hospital—and I don't know if she'll get better. I simply can't tell you how much I love her, and how much I miss her. I haven't a father, or brother or sisters—only my mother. I've never been away from her even for a night till now. I know it sounds silly to you—you'll call me babyish and mother's girl—and so I am, I suppose. But you see, Mother and I haven't had any one but each other—and I'm so terribly, terribly home-sick, and want to be with Mother so much...'

Gladys burst into sobs again, and cried so miserably that Mirabel forgot her own troubles for the moment and put her arm awkwardly round the girl. She saw how little courage Gladys had got—she saw how little she tried to face what had come to her—and she felt a little scornful. But no one could help feeling sorry for the miserable girl. Mirabel had no idea what to do for the best.

'Well,' she said, saying the first thing that came into her head, 'Well, how would you like to be *me*! Sent away from home by your mother and father because they didn't want you, and said you upset your brother and sister and made every one unhappy! That's what *I've* got to put up with! I'm not so lucky as you, I think!'

Gladys raised her head, and for the first time forgot her unhappiness in her scorn of Mirabel.

'*You* unlucky! Don't be silly—you don't know how lucky you are! To have a father *and* a mother, a brother and a sister, all to love and to love you. And I only have my mother and even she is taken away from me! Mirabel, you deserve to be sent away from home if you can't understand that families should love one another! I can tell you, if I had all those people to love *I* wouldn't behave so badly to them that they'd send me away. You ought to be ashamed of yourself.'

Coming from the silent Gladys, this was most astonishing. Mirabel stared into the darkness, not knowing what to say. Gladys got up and went to the door.

'I'm sorry,' she said, in a muffled voice. 'You're unhappy—and I'm unhappy—and I should be sorry for you, and comfort you. But you made your own unhappiness—and I didn't make mine. That's the difference between us.'

The door banged and Mirabel was alone. She sat still in surprise. Who would have thought that Gladys could say all that? Mirabel thought back to her own home. She saw the golden head of her little sister, the dark one of her brother, bent over home-work. She saw the gentle, patient face of her mother, who always gave in to every one. She remembered the good-humoured face of her father, changed to a sad and angry countenance because of her own continual insistence on her own way.

'It was Mother's fault for giving in to me,' she thought. 'And Harry and Joan should have stood up to me. But it's difficult for younger ones to stand up for themselves—and after all, I *am* difficult. I wish I was home now. I'm lonely here, and I've behaved like an idiot. I know Mother would always love me—and yet I've been beastly to her-and turned Daddy against me too. Harry and Joan will be glad I've gone. Nobody in the world wants me or loves me.'

Self-pity brings tears more quickly to the eyes than anything else. Mirabel put her head on the table and wept. She forgot Gladys and her trouble. She only felt sorry for herself. She dried her eyes after a while, and sat up.

'I shall stop behaving badly,' she thought. 'I shall leave

at half-term and go back home and try to do better. I'm tired of being silly. I'll turn over a new leaf tomorrow, and perhaps the girls will feel more friendly.'

She got up and switched on the light. Her watch showed five minutes to nine—almost bed-time. She sat down at the piano and played to herself for a while, and then, when the nine-o'clock bell sounded, made her way upstairs to bed, full of good resolutions. She began to make pictures of how nice the girls would be to her when they found she was turning over a new leaf. Perhaps the twins would find she was somebody worth knowing after all.

Poor Mirabel! When she got into bed that night, she found that she could only get her legs half-way down it! The girls had made a beautiful apple-pie bed, and, not content with that, Elsie had put a spray of holly across the bend of the sheet. Mirabel gave a shout of dismay as the holly pricked her toes.

'Oh! Who's put this beastly thing into my bed? It's scratched my foot horribly!'

Mirabel had never had an apple-pie bed made for her before, She could not imagine what had happened. She tried to force her legs down to the bottom of the bed, but only succeeded in tearing the sheet.

The girls were in fits of laughter. They soon saw that Mirabel had not experienced an apple-pie bed before, and had no idea that the top sheet had been tucked under the bolster, and then folded in half, half-way down the bed, and brought back to fold over the blanket. Doris rolled on her bed in glee, and even placid Anna squealed with joy.

'Golly! You'll have to report that tear to Matron in the morning,' said Elsie, when she heard the sheet torn in half. 'You idiot! You might have guessed that would happen. You'll spend the next sewing-class mending a long rent.'

Mirabel threw the holly at Elsie. She had now discovered what had happened, and was angry and hurt. She got into bed and drew the covers round her. The other chuckled a little and then one by one fell asleep.

In the morning Mirabel awoke early. She lay and thought over what she had decided the night before. It wasn't going to be easy to make a complete change-over but she didn't see anything else to do. She simply could not go on being idiotic. Once you were ashamed of yourself, you had to stop. If you didn't, then you really were an idiot.

So, full of good resolutions still, Mirabel went to her classes. She would work well. She would give Mam'zelle a great surprise. She would please Miss Jenks. She would make up for her rudeness to Miss Quentin. She would even be decent to that wild little Carlotta, and forgive her for that box on the ears. The girls would see she wasn't so bad as they thought she was, and they would turn over a new leaf too, and be friendly to her. Everything would be lovely again—and at the half-term she would leave, and people would be sorry to see her go!

It was with these pleasant thoughts that poor Mirabel entered on a day of horrid shocks and unpleasant surprises!

6   A DAY OF SHOCKS AND SURPRISES

ALISON and Elsie were the two who enjoyed punishing Mirabel more than any of the others. Elsie because she was naturally spiteful, and Alison because she had been so annoyed at losing her turn in Miss Quentin's class.

'I'll sew up the sleeves of Mirabel's coat,' said Alison to Elsie. 'I'll do them awfully tightly. She'll be furious!'

'I'll take out some of her books and hide them,' said Elsie. 'Anna, go and find Mirabel's Wellington boots and put small pebbles inside—right in the toes.'

'Oh, can't some one else do that?' said Anna. 'I shall have to go down to the games-room to get the boots. Bobbie, you go.'

Elsie went to the classroom before morning school and removed various books and exercise papers. There was no one else in the room. The girl spitefully dropped ink on to a maths. paper that Mirabel had done. 'This will teach her to behave better!' said Elsie to herself. 'Now—where shall I put the books?'

She decided to put them at the back of the handwork cupboard, and cover them with the loose raffia there. So into the cupboard went the books, and then Elsie, having a few minutes to spare, looked for something else to do.

She saw the List of Classroom Duties hung up on the wall and went to read them. It was Mirabel's turn that week to keep the vases well-filled with water. Elsie pursed up her lips spitefully.

'I'll empty out the water—and then, when the flowers

begin to droop, Miss Jenks will notice and Mirabel will get kicked off for forgetting the water,' thought Elsie. So out of the window went the water from the four big vases. The flowers were hurriedly replaced just as the first bell went for lessons.

The second form trooped in to take their places. Alison went to hold the door for Miss Jenks. Mirabel took a look round at the girls, hoping to get a smile from some one. She was longing to say that she meant to turn over a new leaf. But nobody looked at her except Elsie, who nudged Anna and then turned away.

'She's coming!' hissed Alison. The class stopped lounging over their desks and talking. They stood up and waited in silence. Miss Jenks was very strict about politeness and good manners in her class.

'Good morning, girls,' said the mistress, putting her books on desk. 'Sit, please. We will... good gracious, Alison, what is that you are wearing on your left wrist?'

'A bracelet,' said Alison, sulkily. The girls looked at it and giggled. It was very like one that Miss Quentin wore. Alison loved to wear anything that even remotely resembled her beloved Miss Quentin's belongings.

'Alison, I am getting tired of asking you to remove bows and brooches and bracelets and goodness knows what,' said Miss Jenks. 'What with putting up with Mirabel's stupidities, and your vanities, I'm going really grey!'

Miss Jenks had flaming red hair, with not a scrap of grey in it. The girls smiled, but were not certain enough of Miss Jenks's temper that day to laugh out loud.

'Bring me that bracelet, Alison,' said Miss Jenks, in a tired voice. 'You can have it back in a week's time providing that during that time I haven't had to remove any other frills and fancies from you.'

Alison sulkily gave up the bracelet. She knew it was the rule that no jewellery should be worn with school uniform, but the little feather-head always trimming herself up with something or other.

'And now please get out your maths. books and the exercise you did for prep. and we will go on to the next page of sums,' said Miss Jenks. 'It's much the same as the one we did yesterday. Work them out, please, and if there is any difficulty, let me know. Come up one by one as I call you, with your maths. exercise paper, and I will correct it at my desk with you.'

The class got busy. Desks were opened and books got out. Pencils were taken from boxes. Exercise books were opened, and there was a general air of getting down to hard work.

Mirabel hunted all through her desk for her maths. book. How curious! It didn't seem to be there. 'Have you borrowed my maths. book she asked Janet in a whisper.

'No whispering,' said Miss Jenks, who had ears like a lynx. 'What is it, Mirabel? One of your usual interruptions. I suppose.'

'No, Miss Jenks,' said Mirabel, meekly. 'I can't find my maths. book, that's all.'

'Mirabel, you're always pretending you can't find this and that,' said Miss Jenks. 'Get your book at once and begin.'

'But, Miss Jenks, it really isn't here,' said Mirabel, hunting frantically through her desk again. The girls nudged one another and grinned. They all knew where it was—at the back of the handwork cupboard. Mirabel might look through her desk all day she wouldn't find her book.

'Share Janet's book, then,' said Miss Jenks, shortly, only half-believing Mirabel. Mirabel heaved a sigh of relief, and opened her arithmetic book to copy down the sums from Janet's text-book. She put ready her maths. paper, which she had done in prep. the night before, to show to Miss Jenks. But as she turned it over the right way, she stared at it in horror. It was covered with ink-spots!

'Just as I've made up my mind to turn over a new leaf, all these things happen!' thought Mirabel in dismay. 'I can't imagine how I got that ink on my paper. Miss Jenks will never believe I didn't know it was there.'

Mirabel was right—Miss Jenks didn't believe it! She looked in disgust at the untidy paper. She would not even correct it.

'Another of your nice little ways, I suppose,' she said. 'Do it again, please.'

'Miss Jenks, I really didn't make all those ink-spots,' said Mirabel. But she had given in too many badly-done papers before, on purpose, for Miss Jenks suddenly to believe her now.

'I don't want to discuss the matter,' said Miss Jenks. 'Do it all again, and let me have it this evening, without any mess on it at all.'

Mirabel went back to her desk. She caught Elsie's spiteful smile, but she did not guess yet that there was a campaign against her. She sat down, angry and puzzled.

The French class came next, and Mirabel discovered, to her dismay, that not only her French books, but also the French paper she had written out the day before as homework, had disappeared. She hunted through her desk again and again, and Mam'zelle grew sarcastic.

'Mirabel, is it possible for you to come out of your desk before the lesson is ended? Soon I shall forget what your face is like.'

'Mam'zelle, I'm sorry, but I can't seem to find the French paper I did yesterday,' said Mirabel, emerging from her desk flushed and worried.

If there was one thing that Mam'zelle could not stand, it

was the non-appearance of any work she had set the class to do. She frowned, and her glasses slid down her big nose. The girls watched gleefully. They knew the signs of gathering wrath. Mam'zelle replaced her glasses on the bridge of her nose.

'Ah, Mirabel! You cannot seem to find the work you did, you say? How many times have I heard that excuse since I have been here at St. Clare's? A thousand times, ten thousand times! You have not done the work. Do not deny it, I know. You are a tiresome girl—you have been tiresome ever since the first day you came. You will always be tiresome. You will give me that work before the end of the morning or you will not play lacrosse this afternoon.'

'But, Mam'zelle, I really *did* do it!' protested Mirabel, almost in tears. 'I can't find my ordinary French books, either. They're gone.'

'Always this Mirabel holds up my class!' cried Mam'zelle, raising her hands to the ceiling and wagging them in a way that made Doris long to imitate her at once. 'She loses things-she looks for them-she makes excuses—I cannot bear this girl.'

'Nor can anybody,' said Alison, delighted at the success of the trick. Mirabel flashed an angry glance at her. She was beginning to wonder if the girls had had any-thing to do with the mysterious disappearance of her things.

'Is's too bad all this happening now,' she thought. 'Mam'zelle might believe me. I really am speaking the truth.'

But Mirabel had so often been silly and untruthful that she had only herself to blame now if no one believed her when she did actually tell truth. She tried once more with Mam'zelle.

'Please do believe me, Mam'zelle,' she begged. 'Elsie saw me doing the paper last night. Didn't you, Elsie?'

'Indeed I didn't,' said Elsie, maliciously.

'Ah, this untruthful Mirabel !' cried Mam'zelle. 'You will do me the paper once because you have not done it- and again you will do it for me because you have told an untruth.'

Mirabel saw her time at break going. She would have to do the two papers then. She looked round the class for sympathy. Usually, comforting glances were sent from one girl to another, when somebody got into trouble. But there were no comforting glances for Mirabel. Every one was glad that the Nuisance was in trouble.

Poor Mirabel! Her troubles were never-ending that morning. Miss Jenks noticed all the drooping flowers in the waterless vases, during the next lesson, and spoke sharply about it.

'Who is Room-Monitor this week?'

'I am,' said Mirabel.

'Well, look at the flowers,' said Miss Jenks. 'It doesn't seem as if they can have a drop of water in the vases, by the look of them.'

'Why, I filled them all up yesterday,' said Mirabel, in- dignantly. 'I did really.'

Miss Jenks went to the nearest vase and tipped it up. 'Not a drop of water,' she said. 'I suppose you will sug- gest next that somebody has emptied all the vases, Mirabel?'

It flashed across the girl's mind that some one might ac- tually have done that, to pay her back for all the annoying thing things she had done. But it seemed such a mean trick– –to make flowers die in order to get somebody into trouble! She flushed and said nothing.

'I suppose you thought I would let you miss part of the lesson whilst you filled up the flowers,' said Miss Jenks, in disgust. 'Hilary, have you finished answering the question on the blackboard? Good—then just go and get some water for the vases, will you?'

Mirabel spent the whole of break doing the French paper twice over. She guessed now, by the grins and nudges among the girls, that most of her troubles were due to them, and she was angry and hurt. 'Just as I had made up my mind to be decent!' she thought, as she wrote out the French papers quickly. 'It's beastly of every one.'

She was late for games because she could not put on her coat in time to go to the field with the others. Alison had sewn up the sleeves well and truly—so tightly that it was impossible to break the stitches. Mirabel had to go and hunt for a pair of scissors to cut the sewn-up sleeves. She was almost in tears.

And then, when she put on her Wellingtons to go across the muddy field-path, she squealed in pain. Nasty little pebbles made her hobble along—and at last she had to stop, take off the boots, and empty the pebbles into the hedge.

Miss Wilton, the sports mistress, had already started the lacrosse game going. 'You're late, Mirabel,' she called. 'Stand aside until half-time. If you can't bother to be in time, you can miss part of the game.'

If was cold standing and watching. Mirabel felt miserable. Everybody and everything was against her. What was the use of trying to be different?

Miss Wilton took her to task at half-time. 'Why were you so late? You know the time perfectly well. You were almost fifteen minutes after the others!'

She waited to hear Mirabel's excuse. The other girls listened. They had not bargained for Miss Wilton enquiring into the matter. Alison felt uncomfortable. She didn't want to get into trouble for sewing up Mirabel's coat-sleeves. She did not want another bad report. Last term's had been very poor, and her father had had a good many things to say that were not pleasant to hear.

Mirabel opened her mouth to pour out her woes—how

her coat-sleeves had been sewn up-stones put into her Wellingtons—and goodness knows what else done to her! Then she shut her mouth again. How often had she scolded her young brother and sister for telling tales of her when she had made things unpleasant for them? She had always said that a tale-bearer was some one quite impossible.

'The girls deserve to have tales told about them,' thought Mirabel, 'but I shan't make myself into some-thing I hate just to get back on them.'

So she said nothing at all.

'Well,' said Miss Wilton, impatiently, 'as you have no excuse, it seems, take off your coat and join in the second half of the game. But next time, if you are late, you will not play in the game at all—you can just go back to school and ask Miss Jenks to give you something to do.'

The game went on. One or two of the girls began to feel uncomfortable. It was decent of Mirabel not to give them away. You couldn't attack people if they behaved well. 'It's time we stopped going for Mirabel,' thought Hilary. 'I'll tell Elsie so tonight!'

7　　A MEETING IN THE COMMON ROOM

ANOTHER meeting, this time called by Hilary, was held that night. It was held in the common room. Every one was there but Mirabel, who was doing her maths paper all over again in the classroom.

'What's the meeting for?' asked Elsie, half-indignant that any one but herself should call a meeting.

'It's about Mirabel,' said Hilary. 'You know she didn't split on us when she had the chance to—so I vote we stop playing tricks on her now. Anyway, we pretty well put her through it today!'

'We're certainly not going to stop,' said Elsie, at once. 'What, stop when she's only just begun to learn her lesson! She'll be as bad as ever if we don't go on showing her we can make things just as tiresome for her as she has made them for us!'

'No, we've done enough,' said Hilary. 'It makes me feel rather mean. I rather wish we hadn't done quite so many things—and anyway, I don't know who spilt ink over her maths. paper, and took the water out of the flowers. We didn't arrange that. Who did it?'

There was a silence. Elsie went red. She did not dare to say she had done anything more than had already been arranged—the others might think her spiteful, or mean.

'I believe it was Elsie!' said Carlotta, suddenly. 'Look how red she's gone!'

Every one looked. Elsie scowled. 'Of course I didn't do anything,' she said. 'I don' t think we did nearly enough. I think a girl who openly says she's jolly well going to make herself too beastly to stay more than half a term ought to be well shown up!'

'Well, she *has* shown up-by her own self!' said Janet. 'No one would have known anything about her or her private affairs if she hadn't gone round yelling them out! I think Hilary is right—we won't do anything more.'

'You talk as if Hilary is head-girl' said Elsie, spitefully.

'Well—so she was in the first form,' said Bobby, losing her temper. 'And let me tell you she was a much better one than you, Elsie.'

'Don't forget that Anna is head-girl too,' said Pat. Anna smiled sleepily. Bobby turned on her at once.

'As if anyone can remember that Anna is head-girl, or anything! What's the good of a head-girl who is always too lazy to do a single thing? We've got two head-girls in this form—and one is spiteful and catty and over-bearing––and the other is fat and lazy!'

'Shut up, Bobby,' said Hilary, uncomfortably. 'It's no good losing your temper like that. Let's get back to the point—and that is, we're not going to persecute Mirabel any more. Let's give her a chance and see if today's lessons have taught her anything. She knows well enough we have all been working against her—and that must be a very horrid experience.'

'Hilary Wentworth—if you don't stop talking as if *you* were head of this form, you'll be sorry,' said Elsie, angered by Bobby's candid speech. 'Anna—for heaven's sake sit up and back me up.'

'But I don't think you're right,' said Anna, in her gentle voice. 'I don't want to persecute Mirabel, either. I don't feel spiteful towards her now.'

'You're too lazy to feel anything,' said Elsie, surprised and furious at Anna's unexpected refusal to back her up. 'You know perfectly well that as head-girls we must work together—and it's an unwritten rule that the form go by what we say.'

'Well, I can't work with you in this,' said Anna. 'I may be fat and lazy and all the other things you probably think about me, and don't say—but I am not catty. So I say, as head-girl of the form—we will NOT continue with our tricks against Mirabel.'

'Well!' said Pat, 'this is going to be difficult—two head-girls, each saying different! I suppose we'd better put it to the vote, which girl we follow. Now—hands up for Anna and doing what she says!'

Every single hand went up at once. Anna grinned and for once sat up really straight. Elsie went white.

'Now—hands up those who wish to follow Elsie,' said Pat. Not a single hand went up, of course. Elsie stood up angrily.

'This is what comes of having to stay down with a lot of half-baked first-formers!' she said, her voice trembling. 'Well—I'll tell you who emptied the water out of the vases––and dropped ink on Mirabel's maths. paper—it was your precious Anna! If you want to follow a girl who does things like that, and then is ashamed to own up to them, well, you can!'

She flung herself out of the room and slammed the door loudly. Anna raised her well-marked eye-brows.

'Well, girls,' she said, in her rather drawling voice, 'I assure you I am not guilty.'

Every one believed her. Anna might be lazy and not bother herself or undertake any kind of responsibility—but at least she was truthful and honest.

'I'm not going to count Elsie as head-girl any more,' said Isabel. 'We'll have only Anna. Come on, Anna—stir yourself, and settle things one way or another.'

'Poor Anna—she will have to open her eyes and wake up at last,' said Carlotta's high voice, rather maliciously. Anna stood up suddenly.

'Well—I'm just as tired of Elsie's spite and cattiness as you are,' she said. 'So if you'll do with just me as head-girl, I'll wake up a bit. It's not been easy trying to work in with Elsie. I'm not going to give her away—but I just can't bear some of the things she says and does. Now—it's not enough just to stop persecuting Mirabel–can't we do something positive—I mean, something to put her right, instead of just stopping her being wrong?'

Every one gaped at Anna. This was the first time the big, sleepy-eyed girl had ever made such a long speech, or suggested anything of her own accord. Hilary thought her suggestion was excellent.

'Yes—that's the way to do things really,' she agreed. 'It's not enough to stop things going wrong—you've got to set them going the way—on the right road. But I don't for the life of me see how. Mirabel is terribly difficult. I can't see that she's any good at anything at all. There isn't anything to work on.'

'She's bad at lessons—no good at games—hopeless at art—poor at gym, said Isabel. 'It there was *some*thing she was good at, we could make it our starting-point—you know, praise her up a bit, and her some self-respect.

Then the second form had great surprise. The Misery-girl spoke, in her rather timid little voice!

'Mirabel is good at something! *Awfully* good!'

Every one stared at Gladys in double-amazement, astonished that she should have spoken at all, and amazed to hear what she said. Gladys seemed to shrink under the gaze of so many pairs of eyes. She wished she had not spoken—but she had been interested, in spite of herself, in the scene that had been going on—and she had suddenly felt that she would like to help stupid Mirabel. After all—she had put her arm round her the night before, and had been kind in her own awkward way.

'What do you mean?' said Anna.

'Well—she's frightfully good at music,' stammered Gladys, horrified now to think she had to speak to so many girls at once.

'How do you know?' asked Janet. 'She's never played any instrument here—and she doesn't even open her mouth in the singing-class.'

'I know because I've heard her,' said Gladys. 'She was in the music-room last night—you know, the one next to the boot-cupboard—and first she played a violin—oh, most beautifully—and then she played the piano. And it was all in the dark too.'

'In the *dark*!' said Carlotta in surprise. 'Whatever were you two doing there in the dark? How queer! Do you usually go and sit in music-rooms in the dark?'

Gladys didn't know what to say. She couldn't confess that she often went to the lonely little music-rooms by herself when she felt extra homesick—the girls would laugh at her, and she couldn't bear that. She stared at Carlotta and said nothing.

'Well, can't you answer?' said Carlotta, impatiently. 'Do you often go and listen to Mirabel playing in the dark?'

'No—of course not,' said Gladys. 'I—I just happened to be there—when Mirabel came in—and she didn't see me. So I heard her playing you see.'

The girls looked at one another. So Gladys disappeared into the dark little music-rooms at night—all alone. What a queer girl she was! They looked at her thin white little face, and two or three of them felt a pang of sympathy for the Misery-girl and her lonely thoughts, whatever they might be. Nobody laughed or teased her about being in the dark in the music-room. Even downright Carlotta made no remark about it.

'You know,' said Janet, looking round at the little company of girls,' Mirabel reminds me in some ways of the O'Sullivan twins!'

'What do you mean?' said Pat, indignantly.

'Well—don't you remember how awfully difficult you were a year ago, when you first came to St. Clare's,' said Janet. 'You just made up your minds to be awkward, and you were! You ought to understand Mirabel's point of view, and be able to tell us how to tackle her. What made you two change your ideas and want to stay here?'

'Oh—as soon as we realized we were acting stupidly — and you were friendly to us—we just sort of settled down and loved everything,' said Pat, trying to remember that first exciting term.

'Right,' said Anna, taking charge of the meeting again.
'That's just what *we'll* do! We think Mirabel was decent
for not splitting on us today—so we'll be friendly towards
her now instead of beastly—and perhaps it we get her to
play to us, and praise her up a bit-she'll settle down too.
What about it ?'

'Yes, Anna!' said every one, Gladys too. Hilary
gazed in surprise at Anna. She would never have
thought that sleepy Anna could have come to the fore
like this—why, she really seemed to be taking a keen interest in everything! And taking the lead too. Perhaps it would
be a good thing that the class had broken away from Elsie's
leadership. Anna seemed as if she was going to take the
chance offered to her by the unexpected quarrel.

'Sh! Here comes Mirabel!' said Pat, as the door opened.
At once the girls began to chatter and gabble about anything that came into their heads. Mirabel looked at them
suspiciously. She felt sure they had been discussing her!
Horrid things. Well—if they had been planning fresh tricks
to play on her, she would go back to her old ways and
upset every single class she could!

8   MIRABEL GIVES THE FORM
A SURPRISE

THE twins talked together that night when they were in
bed. Their beds were next to one another and they could
whisper without any one else hearing what they said.

'We ought to have a few excitements now!' whispered
Pat. 'I bet Elsie won't sit down under this! She'll find

some way of getting back at Anna—and all of us as well!'

'I hope Mirabel will be sensible now,' said Isabel. 'She looked most suspiciously at all of us, I thought and she hardly answered Janet at all when she spoke to her.'

'Well, I'm not surprised, really,' said Pat, with a yawn. 'After all—we did do an awful lot of things to her today. It was funny at first—but I didn't like it much afterwards—even though I must say I think Mirabel deserved a little rough-handling. I say—didn't you think it was funny, Gladys speaking up like that—and admitting she was in the music-room all alone? Funny kid, isn't she?'

'Pat, what Janet said was quite true,' Isabel, speaking rather loudly.

'Sh! Don't speak so loud,' whispered Pat. 'What do you mean?'

'Well, you know—we did behave a little bit like Mirabel —and we did hate it when every one disliked us—it was a miserable feeling,' said Isabel. 'So let's make a bee-line for Mirabel tomorrow, and buck her up a bit. St. Clare's has done a lot for us—let's do a bit for Mirabel.'

'Pat! Isabel! If you don't stop talking at once, I'll report you to Miss Jenks tomorrow!' suddenly came Elsie's sharp voice through the darkness.

'You can't. You're not head-girl,' came Carlotta's cheeky voice, before the twins could answer.

'I'll report you too, for untidy drawers and cupboard,' said Elsie, furiously.

'Well—it will only be the fiftieth time, I should think,' said Carlotta, lazily. 'Go ahead, Miss Catty Elsie!'

There was a delighted squeal of laughter from the dormitory at this. Elsie sat up in bed, furious.

'Carlotta! If you dare to talk like a low-down circus girl to me...,' she began. But at that every one sat up in bed, indignant.

'Listen!' began Bobby, 'any one who calls Carlotta low-down deserves a spanking with a hair-brush! We're all proud of Carlotta—remember how she saved Sadie from being kidnapped last term! It's *you* who are low down, Elsie! Now—just you remember what I said about that hair-brush!'

Elsie was furious. She began to tell Bobby exactly what she thought of her. She forgot to keep her voice low, and when Miss Jenks came along to see that all was quiet in the dormitory, she was amazed to hear a voice going on and on in the darkness—an angry voice, a spiteful voice!

She switched on the light and stood in silence by the door. Every girl was sitting up in bed. Elsie's voice died away in horror. She stared wide-eyed at Miss Jenks.

'Who was that talking just now?' enquired Miss Jenks, in her cool voice.

Nobody answered. Elsie simply could not bear to own up. She swallowed hard, hoping that Miss Jenks would deliver a general lecture and go. Miss Jenks didn't. She just stood and waited.

'Who is in charge of this dormitory?' she asked. 'Oh you, I suppose, Elsie—as you are one of the head-girls for this form. Well—as the culprit does not seem to have enough courage to own perhaps you, as head-girl, will see to it that the girl is punished by going to bed one hour earlier tomorrow. Will you?'

'Yes, Miss Jenks,' answered Elsie, in a very subdued tone. There was a smothered giggle from Carlotta's bed, hurriedly turned into a loud cough.

'You seem to have a cold, Carlotta,' said Miss Jenks, pretending to be quite concerned. 'Perhaps you had better go to Matron tomorrow morning and get a dose of medicine for it.'

'Oh, I shall be quite all right tomorrow morning, Miss Jenks, thank you,' Carlotta hurriedly assured her.

'Good night, girls,' said Miss Jenks, and switched off the light. As soon as her footsteps had died away, the girls began to giggle and whisper.

'Elsie! See that you put yourself to bed an hour earlier tomorrow!' whispered Carlotta.

Elsie lay in bed, her cheeks burning. Why hadn't she owned up? Then she wouldn't have been so humiliated! She jolly well wouldn't go to bed early the next night, anyway. She shut her ears with her fingers, so as not to hear what the girls were whispering. She did not dare to tell them to stop—and as for threatening to report them—well, that would make them laugh all the more!

Every one felt scornful of Elsie—but they also thought the whole thing was funny. The girls were quite determined that Elsie *should* go to bed early the next night. They were not going to let her off the punishment she had meekly promised to give to wreak on the culprit!

The next day the twins gave Mirabel a cheerful grin at the breakfast-table. She smiled back, surprised and warmed. She had been expecting a few more tricks, and the unexpected smile surprised her very much.

After breakfast Pat and Isabel spoke to Mirabel. 'Did you hear about the row in our dormitory last night?' asked Pat.

'I knew there was something up,' said Mirabel. 'I heard the others talking about it. What was it?'

The twins told Mirabel about Elsie and Miss Jenks, and the girl smiled. 'Thanks for telling me,' she said, 'It was funny. I say—is the form going to do beastly things to me today? You know, I'd just decided to turn over a new leaf—when you did all those things.'

'Had you really decided to change?' said Pat, in surprise. 'Well—don't worry—we're not going to get back at you any more. But for goodness' sake do your bit too. It's pretty sickening having class after class upset, you know.

You may feel in a temper about your home-affairs—but that really isn't any reason for venting your temper on the class!'

'No—I see that now,' said Mirabel. 'I'm an idiot—always have been. Well—I bet you'll be glad to see the back of me at half-term.'

'Wait and see,' said Isabel. 'I say—our form is giving a concert next week, in aid of the Red Cross. Every one is to do something. Could you play the violin for us, do you think? And perhaps the piano too?'

'How do you know I play?' asked Mirabel, in surprise. But at that moment Miss Jenks bustled the whole class off for a nature-walk, and Mirabel found herself walking with the timid Gladys, who, remembering the night in the dark music-room, felt afraid to say a word. Mirabel felt awkward too, so the two hardly exchanged a single word.

The twins, when the chance came, hurriedly told the rest of the form that they had asked Mirabel to play at the concert planned for the following week. Every form had been asked to get up something in aid of the Red Cross, and this was to be the second form's contribution.

'Did she say she would?' asked Bobby.

"No—but we'll put her name down on the programme,' said Pat. 'I bet she will! She was quite nice this morning.'

Mirabel found her books back in her desk that day. Anna had taken them from their hiding-place and put them back. Elsie had scowled, but had said nothing. She didn't know whom she hated most—Anna—or that saucy Carlotta!

When the programme for the Red Cross concert was drawn up that evening, Isabel called across to Mirabel.

'Hie, Mirabel! I've put you down for a violin solo, and a piano solo. What will you play? Can you tell us the names of the pieces?'

'I haven't my violin here,' said Mirabel, hesitatingly.

'Pooh—you can easily send a telegram home for it,' said Pat. 'And Anna will lend you hers to practise on this week—won't you, Anna?'

'Of course,' said Anna. 'I'll go and get it now and you can see if you like the feel of it. It's a good one.'

Anna went to fetch to fetch her violin. She took it out of its case and put it into Mirabel's hands. As she had said, it was a good one. Mirabel drew the bow across it lovingly.

'Play something,' said Isabel. And then, as in the dark music-room, Mirabel played some of the melodies she loved. She forgot the girls in the common room, she forgot St. Clare's, she forgot herself. She was a real little musician, and she put all her heart into the music she loved.

The girls listened spell-bound. Two or three girls in the school played the violin very well—but Mirabel made it speak. The notes rang out pure and true, and Anna was amazed that her violin could produce such music.

When Mirabel stopped, every one clapped frantically. 'I say! You *are* marvellous!' said Pat, her eyes shining. 'Golly—you'll make every one sit up at the concert next week, I can tell you. Now go and play something on the piano. Go on. You simply must!'

Mirabel looked round at the admiring audience, with flushed cheeks and bright eyes. Only Elsie Fanshawe did not applaud. She sat at a table, reading a book, taking no notice at all.

'Go on, Mirabel—play us something on the piano!' insisted Pat.

Mirabel went across to the old piano in the common room. It was there for the girls to strum on if they wanted to. Usually dance music or popular songs were hammered out on it—but tonight something quite different was played!

Mirabel's long, sensitive fingers ran over the notes, and one of Chopin's nocturnes filled the quiet common room. Most of the girls loved good music, and they listened in delight. Gladys shut her eyes. Music always stirred her very much, though she learnt no instrument, and knew little about it.

The notes died. The girls sat up, pleased. 'Look here —play that at the concert next week,' said Hilary. 'It's heavenly. I heard it on the wireless in the hols—but you play it much better!'

'I don't,' said Mirabel, red with embarrassment and pleasure. 'All right—I'll play it. And if you really want me to play something on the violin too I'll send a telegram tomorrow asking for my own violin to be sent. Anna's is a lovely one—but I'm more at home with my own.'

'Good,' said Isabel. 'I say—aren't you a dark horse - never saying a word about your music—keeping it up your sleeve like that! You've got a real gift. I wish I had a gift. You're lucky!'

Mirabel went to help Isabel to draw up the programme. Her words echoed in her mind. 'You've got a real gift!' She remembered Miss Theobald's words too. 'Difficult children often have some hidden quality— some gift—something to make them worth-while!'

Nobody at home thought her worth-while—or surely they wouldn't have sent her away! But she was worth-while! See how the girls loved hearing her play. It was a pity she hadn't accepted her father's offer to learn music at St. Clare's. She had no other gift but music, and she had refused to develop that, out of obstinacy.

'I bet you could pass any music exam. you went in for,' said Isabel, handing Mirabel a few programmes to print. 'Nobody in our form is specially good at music. It's pity you don't learn. You would be a credit to us—you'd make some of the top-formers sit up, I bet! And I guess you'd win the music-prize.'

'Well—I'll certainly send that telegram tomorrow,' said Mirabel, printing the programmes neatly. She felt happy for the first time that term. It was nice to be working in friendliness with some one like Isabel. It was lovely to be praised for something. Nobody thought a great deal of her music at home, because none of them were musical— except her brother—and dear me, how she snubbed him! Mirabel felt annoyed with herself when she remembered that. She ought to have encouraged him.

'I really must have been tiresome,' she thought. 'Well —going away from home does make you see things clearly. When I go back at half-term I'll show them I'm not as bad as they think!'

That night, at eight o'clock all the second form winked at one another. If Elsie was going to bed an hour earlier, it was time she went. But she showed no sign. She had come back from supper and had settled down to read again, saying nothing to anybody.

'Bedtime for little girls!' said Carlotta. Elsie took no notice.

'Naughty girls must go to bed early,' said Bobby, loudly. Elsie did not move.

The girls looked at one another. It was quite clear that Elsie was not going to get up and go. She had not only been afraid to own up to Miss Jenks the night before —but she was now going to evade the punishment!

To every one's surprise Anna spoke. 'Elsie!' she said. 'You know perfectly well what you have to do. Don't make us all ashamed of you.'

'You can't talk to *me* like that!' said Elsie, turning over a page.

'I can,' said Anna, calmly. 'I am head-girl of the form. I have the right to tell you what to do.'

'You haven't,' said Elsie, furiously. 'I'm head-girl too.'

'You're not, you're not!' cried a dozen voices. 'We only recognize Anna as head-girl now. We don't want you!'

'Only Miss Jenks can decide a thing like that,' said Elsie, looking round at the girls.

'Perhaps you are right,' said Anna, in her slow voice. 'Come with me and we will let Miss Jenks decide.'

Hilary looked at Anna in admiration. She knew that this was the one thing that would defeat Elsie. On no account would Elsie go to Miss Jenks at the moment! It would be far too humiliating.

Elsie hesitated. The girls waited. They knew Elsie would not consent to go with Anna. Anna stood up as if she was going.

'I'm not going to Miss Jenks,' said Elsie, in low voice.

'I thought not,' said Anna, and sat down again. 'Well —either Miss Jenks decides this matter or the girls do. I don't mind.'

'*We*'ll decide—we've already decided!' said Janet. 'Anna is our head-girl, and we don't want Elsie. And that being so, Elsie—you'll just do as Anna says, and go off to bed. It's your own silly fault.'

That was too much for Elsie. Her obstinacy rose up and she pursed her thin lips. 'I'm not going ,' she said. 'I'm not obeying Anna. She may be your head-girl—but I won't admit she's mine!'

'Right,' said Carlotta, cheerfully, getting up. 'Come on, Bobby-Janet-twins. Get hold of Elsie, and we'll bump her all the way upstairs to bed! We can't have her disobeying Miss Jenks's orders like this! My word—won't the third form stare when we go by with poor Elsie!'

'No—don't!' cried Elsie, in dismay jumping to her feet. She knew the wild little Carlotta would stop at nothing. 'I'll go. I'll go. But I hate you all!'

She burst into tears, and with loud sobs went to the door. Carlotta sat down. When Elsie had gone, she looked round.

'I didn't really mean us to bump her up the stairs to bed,' she said,' but I guessed she'd go of her own accord if I suggested it.'

'She'll be awful tomorrow,' said Bobby. Anna shook her big head.

'No,' she said. 'I know Elsie. She will begin to feel a martyr, and terribly sorry for herself. She will try to get our sympathy by being subdued and meek.'

'Yes—I think you're right,' said Janet. 'Well—the best thing is not to take any notice of her at all. We don't want to get spiteful—just let's leave her alone and take no notice at all.'

'That's the best thing,' said Anna. She took up her knitting again. 'Oh dear—being the only head-girl is very wearing. There seem so many things to decide!'

9   ANNA SEES THE
HEAD-MISTRESS

THE next morning Mirabel wanted to send her telegram. Anna told her what to do.

'You'll have to go and get permission from Miss Theobald. Then you can slip down into the town with some-body after morning school,' she said. 'I'll go with you if you like.'

Mirabel went to ask permission. She knocked at Miss Theobald's door and was told to come in. The Head Mistress looked up. She did not smile.

'What is it, Mirabel?' she asked.

'Please, Miss Theobald, may I send a telegram home?' asked Mirabel.

Still Miss Theobald did not smile or unbend in any way. She looked really stern. Mirabel began to feel very uncomfortable.

'What is the telegram about?' she asked. 'You know that you cannot leave before half-term. There is no sense in upsetting your household with telegrams.'

'It's nothing to do with my leaving,' said Mirabel. 'It's—it's—well, Miss Theobald, I just want to ask my mother if she'll send my violin, that's all.'

The head looked surprised. 'Your violin? she said. 'Why? You don't learn music, do you?'

'No,' said Mirabel. 'I wish I did now. But I wouldn't when Daddy gave me the chance. You see—the second form are giving a concert for the Red Cross next week— and I said I would play for them. I'd like my own violin to play. It's a beauty.'

Miss Theobald looked at Mirabel. 'So you *have* a

gift, Mirabel!' she said. 'You remember what I said to you? I wonder if there is anything worth-while in you after all!'

Mirabel went red. She stood on first one foot and then on another. She felt certain that Miss Theobald had had bad reports of her from every mistress.

'I'm not sure that I shall let you ask for your violin,' said Miss Theobald at last. 'I hear that you misbehave at practically every class. You try to spoil everything, it seems. How do I know that you will behave at the concert?'

'I will,' said Mirabel, earnestly. 'You won't believe me, perhaps—but I've turned over a new leaf now. I've got tired of being silly.'

'I see,' said Miss Theobald. 'You've stopped misbehaving just because you're tired of it—not because you're ashamed of it, or want to do better, or want us to think well of you. Only just because you're tired of it. You disgust me, Mirabel. Go, please. I'm disappointed in you. I had hoped that possibly you might turn over a new leaf for some better motive. I thought I saw some courage in you, some real intelligence that might help you to realize your foolishness and selfishness in behaving as you did. Now I see that you have none—you only stop because you yourself are tired of misbehaviour, and, possibly, are tired also of having the others unfriendly towards you. Please go.'

Mirabel was struck with horror at the cold, stern words. She had felt so pleased with herself to think she was turning over a new leaf. She *had* been ashamed of herself. She hadn't only got tired of being silly. She opened her mouth to defend herself, but the sight of Miss Theobald's stern face frightened her. She went out of the room without a word.

Miss Theobald sat and thought for a few minutes.

Then she rang her bell. 'Ask Miss Jenks to come to me for a few minutes,' she told the maid.

Miss Jenks soon appeared. 'Sit down for a moment,' said Miss Theobald. 'I want to talk to you about Mirabel Unwin. I have had continual bad reports from you about her. Is there any improvement at all?'

'Yes,' said Miss Jenks at once. 'She seems suddenly to be settling down. I don't quite know why. Has anything happened? I saw her just now, and she looked as if she had been crying.'

'Probably she had,' said Miss Theobald, and told Miss Jenks what had just passed between her and Mirabel.

'I should like to know if the girl has suddenly changed for the right reasons, or the wrong ones,' she said. 'Perhaps the head-girls could tell me. Send them, will you?'

'There seems to be some sort of upset between the two head-girls of my form,' said Miss Jenks. 'I don't think Elsie Fanshawe has gone down very well with the first-formers who came up into my form. But Anna seems unexpectedly to be showing some signs of responsibility and leadership. I'll go and send the two girls to you. Perhaps they can tell you more about Mirabel. Personally I think we might give her a chance now, and let her have her violin.'

She left the room and went to find Anna and Elsie. They were in the common room with the others. As the door opened and Miss Jenks appeared all the girls rose to their feet and stopped chattering. Janet turned off the wireless.

'Miss Theobald wants the two head-girls to go to her for a few minutes,' said Miss Jenks in her cool voice. 'Will you go to at once, please?'

She left the room. There was a silence. Anna stood up to go. So did Elsie. But quick as thought Carlotta pulled her down again to her chair.

'You're not head-girl, Elsie. You know you're not. We won't have you—and if we won't have you, then Anna is the only head-girl. You are not going to Miss Theobald!'

'Don't be an idiot!' snapped Elsie, scrambling up again. 'You know I've got to go. I can't tell Miss Theobald I'm no longer head-girl.'

'Well, Anna can,' said Hilary. 'It's unfortunate, Elsie—but we all happen to think the same about this. You were a bad head-girl—and we won't accept you. You wouldn't let Miss Jenks decide it—you've got to abide by it. Anna must go alone.'

'She's not to, she's not to,' said Elsie, half-crying. 'It's shameful. What will Miss Theobald think?'

'You should have thought of these things before,' said Hilary. 'Anna, go. Say as little as you can about Elsie, of course—but please let it be understood that you are the only head-girl of the second form now.'

Anna went. Elsie saw that the whole of the second form would stop her by force if she tried to follow. So she lay back in her chair, looking as forlorn and miserable as she could, letting the tears trickle down her cheeks. She hoped that girls would feel uncomfortable, and very sorry. But nobody did. In fact, they took no notice of her at all, and went on cheerfully chattering among themselves. It was Saturday morning, and except for an hour's lesson, they were free to do as they chose.

Mirabel was not there. She had had a shock, and it had upset her very much. She did not want anyone to see that she had been crying, so she had gone to the cloakroom to bathe her eyes. She came out of the room just as Anna passed it on her way to the Head. Anna spoke to her.

'Hallo! Did you get permission from the Head to send for your violin? I'll come down to the post-office with you if you like.'

'I didn't get permission,' said Mirabel, miserably. 'Anna, Miss Theobald was awful to me. She thinks I've only turned over a new leaf because I was tired of being an idiot. But I haven't. I'm awfully ashamed of myself now. It was dreadful having you all doing beastly things—and now even Miss Theobald is against me. What's the use of trying? It's just no good at all. I shan't play at the concert. I shan't do anything.'

Anna stared at Mirabel, surprised. 'Look here, I can't wait now,' she said. 'I've been sent for by the Head. But I'll have a talk with you afterwards, see? I'm awfully sorry, Mirabel. Really I am. Cheer up.'

She ran down the passage to Miss Theobald's drawing room and knocked.

'Come in!' said Head's pleasant voice. Anna entered, half-scared. Miss Theobald was kind and just—but her wisdom and dignity awed every girl, and it was quite an ordeal to go for any kind of interview.

'Good morning, Anna,' said Miss Theobald. 'Where is Elsie Fanshawe?'

'Elsie isn't head-girl now, Miss Theobald,' said Anna, feeling awkward. Miss Theobald looked most surprised.

'I hadn't heard this,' she said. 'Why isn't she?'

'We all decided that she wasn't quite fit to be at present,' said Anna, finding it difficult to explain without giving Elsie away too much.

'Miss Jenks knows nothing of this,' said the Head. 'Why didn't you ask her advice?'

'Elsie didn't want us to,' said Anna. 'She said she would rather accept our decision, without us taking matters any further. It's—it's rather difficult to explain, Miss Theobald, without telling tales.'

'Did Hilary Wentworth and the O'Sullivan twins agree to this?' asked the Head. She had great faith in the fairness and common sense of these three girls.

'Oh yes,' said Anna. 'I wouldn't have done it myself—I'm too lazy, I'm afraid. But once the girls wanted me to accept responsibility and carry on without Elsie, I had to take it.'

'Of course,' said Miss Theobald, sensing in Anna something better and stronger than she had known before in the lazy slow-moving girl. 'Well—I won't ask any more questions, Anna. I think probably the second form are right—all I hope is that some good will come out of this for Elsie. I can see an improvement in *you* already!'

Anna blushed. Responsibility was a nuisance—but it did bring definite rewards, not the least of which was an added self-respect.

'Anna, I sent for you because I want to ask you about Mirabel Unwin,' said Miss Theobald. 'I always take the head-girl of any form into my confidence, as you know. Will you tell me what your opinion is of Mirabel—whether it is bad or good—anything that can help me in dealing with her. You know all the details as to why she was sent here because she has told the whole school!'

Anna seldom wasted words. She said shortly what Miss Theobald wanted to know. 'Mirabel has been awfully tiresome, and the second form punished her for it. She's ashamed of herself now—and she wants to show us she's some good. Could you let her send for her violin?'

'Very well,' said Miss Theobald, smiling at Anna's directness. 'I refused her permission a little while ago. Will you, as head-girl, tell her I have changed my mind, and she can go down and send off the telegram. Tell her too, that I shall like to hear her play at the second form concert.'

'Yes, Miss Theobald,' said Anna. 'Thank you.' The girl left the room, pleased. For the first time in her lazy life she felt that she had some importance. The Head had sent for her and actually listened to her. It was worth making an effort, if people like Miss Theobald appreciated it.

She went to look for Mirabel. She found her in the common room, reading rather soberly, her eyes still red.

'Mirabel! Come on down to the post-office and send that telegram,' said Anna. 'Miss Theobald says you may. And she says she will look forward to hearing you play at the concert next week.'

Mirabel looked up, astonished and delighted. This was a lovely surprise after having her hopes dashed and her good resolutions misunderstood. she stood up, glowing.

'Anna! It's because of you Miss Theobald said I could send the telegram. Thanks awfully. You're a brick.'

'It wasn't altogether me,' said Anna. 'Hurry up and get your coat on. We haven't much time.'

They hurried down to the post-office. The telegram was sent off—and caused much surprise in Mirabel's home!

'She wants her violin!' said her mother, in astonishment. 'Why, she must be settling down a bit. I *am* glad!'

So the violin was packed up, registered and sent off at once. It arrived on the Monday of the week following, and Mirabel unpacked it joyfully. Her own violin! Now she would be able to play beautifully. She would show the second form what real music was!

'And I'll astonish Miss Theobald a bit too,' thought Mirabel. 'She'll see I have a real gift—even if I haven't anything else! I'd like her to think I was worth-while—I really would.'

GLADYS IS SURPRISING

THE second form were very busy preparing for their concert. They were going to charge sixpence for the tickets, and all the first form, most of the third form, and even a few of the higher form girls had promised to come. All the mistresses had promised too. It was to be quite a big affair.

The girls were to manage everything themselves. They prepared the programmes and the tickets. Isabel drew a fine big poster and coloured it. She put it up in the big assembly room where every one could see it.

The concert was to be held in the gym, where there was a fine platform. The second form grew quite excited about it. Too excited for Mam'zelle's liking. She could not bear to feel that the class were thinking about something else in her lessons.

'Isabel! Pat! Did you not sleep last night, that you dream so this morning? What was the question I have just asked the class?'

The twins stared at Mam'zelle in alarm. Neither of them had heard the question. Carlotta whispered softly.

'She said, "Has anyone here seen my glasses?"' whispered Carlotta, grinning. This was quite untrue, as everyone knew! But the twins fell into the trap at once. They stared innocently at Mam'zelle, seeing her glasses perched as usual on her big nose.

'Well?' said Mam'zelle, sharply. 'What did I ask the class?'

'You asked if we had seen your glasses anywhere,' said Pat. 'But they are on your nose, Mam'zelle.'

There was a squeal of laughter from the class. Mam'zelle banged on her desk angrily. '*Ah, que eles abominable*!' she cried. '*Insupportable*!'

The twins glared at Carlotta, who was holding her sides. She shook her head at them, tears of laughter in her eyes. 'Wait till break, you wretch!' said Pat.

'*Taisez-vous*!' said Mam'zelle. 'Pat! Isabel! Of what were you thinking just now when I addressed the class? Be truthful!'

'Well, Mam'zelle—I was thinking of the concert our form is holding on Saturday,' said Pat. 'I'm sorry. My thoughts just wandered away.'

'So did mine,' said Isabel.

'If they wander away again I shall not come to the concert,' threatened Mam'zelle. There was a loud and universal groan.

'We shan't hold the concert unless you come!'

'You *must* come, Mam'zelle! You laugh louder than any one!'

'I will come if you write me a nice composition,' said Mam'zelle, suddenly beaming again. 'You shall write me a beautiful essay and tell me all that is to happen at this wonderful concert. With no mistakes at all. That will please me greatly. That shall be your prep. for tomorrow.'

The girls groaned again. French essays were awful to do—and this one would be difficult. Anyway, the idea had put Mam'zelle into a better temper, so that was something!

Two girls were doing nothing in the concert at all. Elsie had refused to do anything, and had announced her intention of not even coming. And nobody had asked the little Misery-girl to do anything. Every one felt certain that Gladys would not and could not do a thing. They thought it would be kinder to leave her out altogether.

Gladys was hurt because she was not asked, yet glad that she was not pressed to do anything. She shut more

Isabel painted a big poster for the concert

and more up into herself, only spoke when she was spoken to, and was so quiet in every lesson that the teachers hardly knew she was there. Only in Miss Quentin's class did she show any real animation. Not that Miss Quentin ever asked her to act a part, because, like everyone else, Miss Quentin always passed over Gladys, thinking that such a little mouse could never do anything!

But Gladys watched the others acting, and for once in a way forgot to brood over her troubles when she saw Bobby strutting across the room as a king of duke, and Carlotta playing the part of a jester.

Alison adored Miss Quentin's classes. She really did work hard in those—harder than she worked in any one else's. For one thing she was pretty and graceful, and parts such as princesses or fairies were given naturally to her, and for another thing, she lived for Miss Quentin's words of praise. She thought Quentin was 'just wonderful!'

The preparations for the concert went on well. Doris was to give some of her clever imitations. She meant to mimic Mam'zelle, who had all kinds of mannerisms which were a joy to the class. She meant to imitate Clara, the cook, a jolly, rough-ready person much liked by the girls. And she meant to dress up as Matron, and imitate her doling out advice and medicine to various girls.

'Doris, you really are a scream,' said Bobby, enjoying the girl's clever performance in rehearsal. 'You ought to be on the stage.'

'I'm going to be a doctor,' said Doris.

'Oh—well, you'll be a jolly good one because you'll make all your patients scream with laughter!' said Bobby.

Every one was doing something—either reciting, playing the piano or violin, singing or dancing—every one, that is except Elsie and Gladys. Carlotta was going to give a display of acrobatics. She was marvellous at such circus tricks as turning cart-wheels, walking on her hands and so on.

'You and Doris, Carlotta, will be the hits of the evening,' said Pat. She and Isabel were going to give a dialogue, supposed to be funny, but they both felt it was not nearly so good as any one else's contribution. Bobby was to do conjuring tricks! She was very good at these, and had lot of idiotic patter that fell from her lips in a never-ending torrent.

'I bet Mirabel will be a hit too,' said Janet, after the girl had played her concert piece to them, during rehearsal. 'Good thing we found out she could play!'

'By the way—how *did* you find out?' asked Mirabel, putting her violin into its case. 'I kept meaning to ask you. I didn't think anybody knew.'

'Yes—somebody did,' said Janet, looking round to see if Gladys was in the room; but she was not. 'It was Gladys who told us.'

'*Gladys*!' said Mirabel, suddenly remembering the night in the dark music-room. 'Yes—of course—she heard me that night.'

'She said you were in the dark,' said Pat. 'So that means she was too. Funny kid, isn't she, sitting about in dark rooms all by herself. She really is a little misery I can't think what's the matter with her. She never tells anyone. If she did, we might help her a bit—get a smile out of her occasionally, or something.'

'Oh—she told me what's the matter,' said Mirabel, remembering everything Gladys had said.

'*Did* she?' said Bobby, in surprise. 'Well, what is the matter with her?'

'It's her mother,' said Mirabel. 'She's in hospital— awfully ill—perhaps she's going to die. Gladys said she's only got her mother—no father or brothers or sister—and they were sort of all-in-all to one another. She'd never been away from her mother even for a night till she was sent here when her mother went to hospital. She said she was awfully homesick, and missed her mother terribly. I suppose she thinks every day she may hear bad news or something.'

The girls heard all this in silence. They felt sorry and uncomfortable. The little Misery-girl really did have something to worry about. Everyone there but Carlotta had mothers they loved—and fathers—and most of them had brothers and sister. Even slow-minded Anna, who had little imagination, knew for one moment the sort of heartache that Gladys carried with her day and night.

'Why didn't you tell us this?' asked Bobby.

'I didn't remember it till now,' said Mirabel.

'Well, I think you should have told us at once,' said Hilary. 'We might have been decenter to Gladys. She's a poor little thing, without any courage or spunk—but we haven't exactly made things any easier for her. You really are to blame for not having told us, Mirabel.'

Mirabel was really conscience-stricken. She couldn't think how she could have forgotten Gladys's trouble. She had been so wrapped up in her own, and then, when the girls had become friendly and helped her, she had been so happy that she had not given a thought to the little Misery-girl. She stared unhappily at Hilary.

'I'm sorry,' she said. 'I *should* have told you. All the same, I don't think Gladys would like it if she knew that everyone knew about her troubles. So don't tell her you know. Just be nice to her and notice her a bit.'

The second form received this advice in silence. Mirabel sensed that they did not think very much of her for forgetting another person's troubles. She said no more, but went off to put her violin away.

'I wonder where Gladys is,' she thought. 'I've a good a mind to hunt for her and ask her if she's heard any news of her mother lately. After all, it might help a bit if someone shares the news with her.'

Mirabel went to look for Gladys. She could not seem to find the girl anywhere. It was puzzling.

'Well, she simply *must* be somewhere!' said Mirabel to herself. 'I wonder if she's up in the boxrooms. I saw her coming down from there the other day and wondered whatever had taken her there.'

She went up the stairs to the top of the school. Trunks and bags were kept in the attics, but little else. There was a light showing under the door of one of the attics—and from the room came a voice.

It didn't sound like Gladys's voice. It was deep and strong. Mirabel listened in surprise. The voice was declaiming one of the speeches in *The Tempest*, which the second form were taking that term with Miss Jenks.

'That's not Gladys,' thought Mirabel. 'I wonder who it is. Ah—now there's a different voice. There must be two or three people there. But who can they be? Only the second form are doing *The Tempest* this term—and all but Gladys were at rehearsal this evening.

A third voice spoke, gentle and feminine. Mirabel could bear it not longer. She really must see who the speakers were. They were declaiming Shakespeare's words beautifully.

She opened the door. The voice stopped at once. Mirabel stared into the room, expecting to see three or four people there, rehearsing the play. But there was only one person there—Gladys!

'Golly! It's only you!' said Mirabel, in astonishment.

'I thought there must be lots here. I heard all kinds of different voices. Was it *you*?'

'Yes,' said Gladys. 'Go away. Can't I even do this in peace?'

'What are you doing?' asked Mirabel, going into the room and shutting the door. 'Do tell me. It sounded fine. Do you know it all by heart?'

'Yes, I do,' said Gladys. 'I love acting. I always have. But Miss Quentin never gives me a chance in the Drama class. I could act the parts well. I know I could. You see me act Bobby's part in that play we're doing with Miss Quentin!'

And before Mirabel's astonished eyes, the girl began to act the part that had been given to Bobby. But she acted it superbly. She *was* the part! The little Misery-girl faded, and another character came into the attic, someone with a resonant voice, a strong character, and a fierce face. It was extraordinary.

Mirabel stood and gaped. Her astonishment and admiration were so plain that Gladys was impelled to show her another part in the play—Carlotta's part. Here again she was twice as good as the fiery Carlotta, and her voice, wild and strong, quite different from Gladys's usual meek, milk-and-water voice, rang through the attic.

'Gladys! You're simply marvellous!' said Mirabel. 'You're to come and show the girls. Come on. Come on downstairs at once. I never saw anything like it in my life. *You* to act like that! Who would have thought it? You're such a mouse, and your voice is so quiet—and yet, when you act, you're Somebody, and you quite frighten me. You simply *must* come down and show the girls what you do.'

'No,' said Gladys, becoming herself again and looking half the size she had seemed two minutes before.

'Oh, Gladys,' said Mirabel, suddenly remembering why she had been looking for the girl. 'Gladys—how's your mother? I do hope you've got good news.'

'Thank you—it's just about the same,' said Gladys. 'Mother can't even write to me, she's so ill. If I could just get a letter from her, it would be something!'

'Does she get *your* letters?' asked Mirabel.

'Of course,' said Gladys. 'I keep telling her how much I miss her, and how lonely and unhappy I am without her.'

'But, Gladys—how silly!' said Mirabel.

'What do you mean?' asked Gladys, half indignantly. 'Mother wants to know that.'

'I should have thought she would have been much gladder to think you were trying to settle down and be happy,' said Mirabel. 'It must make her very miserable indeed to feel you are so lonely and sad. I should think it would make her worse.'

'It won't,' said Gladys, her eyes filling with tears. 'If she thought I was happy here, and getting other interests, she would think I was forgetting her.'

'I do think you're silly, Gladys,' said Mirabel, wishing she was Hilary or Anna, so that she might know the best way of tackling some one like Gladys. 'Don't you want your mother to be proud of you? She'll think you are an awful coward—no spunk at all—just giving in like this, and weeping and wailing.'

'Oh, you *are* hateful!' cried Gladys. 'As if my mother would ever think things like that of me, ever! Go away. I won't come down with you. And don't you dare to tell any one what you saw me doing. It's my secret. You'd no right to come spying like that. Go away.'

Mirabel looked at Gladys's angry little face, and wondered what to do or say. She hadn't done any good, that was certain. 'I suppose I haven't got the character to help people properly, like Hilary or Anna,' thought Mirabel, going soberly downstairs. 'I've got a lot to learn. When I go home at half-term next week, I'll really try and do better.'

She went down to the library to get a book. But, as she
hunted through the shelves, she kept thinking of Gladys.
She couldn't just do nothing. If she, Mirabel, couldn't help
Gladys, maybe somebody else could. Hilary could. She
was always so sensible. So was Bobby—and the twins,
too. She would go and tell them what had happened, and
leave it to them to do what they could. Mirabel was beginning to have a very low opinion of herself and her powers.

She left the library and went to find Hilary. She was
lucky enough to see her in a music-room with Bobby,
Janet and the twins, practising something for the concert. Good! This was just the chance to tell them what
had happened!

11   A DISAPPOINTMENT FOR
THE SECOND FORM

'I SAY!' said Mirabel, opening the door. 'Can I interrupt
a moment?'

'I suppose so,' said Bobby. 'What's up?'

'It's about Gladys,' said Mirabel, and she told them how
she had found the girl acting all by herself in the boxroom.
Then she went on to tell them what she had said to Gladys,
and how had failed to help her—only made her angry.

'Well,' said Hilary, listening intently. 'I think, Mirabel,
you gave Gladys some very sound advice. Really I do. Of
course Gladys ought to stop moaning to her mother. She
must find a little pluck somewhere, or she'll go to pieces.

You did right to say that it would help her mother if she knew Gladys was settling down, and trying to do well.'

'Oh—I'm glad you think that,' said Mirabel. 'I'm not so good as you are at knowing what to do for the best for people. By the way—Gladys said she didn't want me to tell everybody.'

'Well, you haven't,' said Hilary. 'You've only told us five—and we understand perfectly. But, Mirabel, as it seems that Gladys has taken you into her confidence and nobody else, I think you'd better go on tackling the matter!'

'Yes!' said all the others.

'Oh *no*,' said Mirabel, horrified. 'I came to ask you to help. I'm no good at this sort of thing.'

'Well, it's time you were,' said Hilary, firmly. 'Now come on, Mirabel—we all tried to help you when you needed it—you've got to do the same to Gladys. Be friends with her, and buck her up—and if you can persuade her to show us how she can act, we'll all listen and applaud— and she must be in the concert!'

'She can't be. It's the day after tomorrow, and all the programmes are written out,' objected Isabel. 'We really can't write them all out again.'

'She wouldn't want to be in the concert, anyhow,' said Mirabel. 'All right, Hilary—I'll do what I can. But I really am very bad at this sort of thing.'

It was distasteful to Mirabel to mention the matter to Gladys again. She always felt awkward at anything involving fact or understanding in another's troubles. She would very much rather have left it to the others. Still, once she said she would do a thing, she did it.

Gladys was surprised, and not too pleased to find Mirabel always at her elbow the next day. 'Gladys, I didn't mean to make you angry,' Mirabel said, when they were alone for a few minutes. 'I'm clumsy in what I say. I know

I am. But I really and truly am sympathetic. I don't expect I can help at all—but I'd like to.'

'Well,' said Gladys, looking at Mirabel's earnest face, 'I was angry yesterday. Nobody likes being told they're cowardly. But I thought it all over and in some ways I think you're right. I shouldn't keep writing to my mother and telling her how miserable and lonely I am. I know it would worry her—and that might keep her from getting well.'

'Yes, it might,' said Mirabel, pleased that what she had said had, after all, had some effect on Gladys. 'I say—look here—wouldn't she be *thrilled* if she knew you were in the concert—acting like that—being clapped by everybody! I do wish you'd let the girls see you act.'

Gladys hesitated. She did know, quite certainly, that her mother would be pleased to hear of any success she made—but she was such a mouse, so afraid of everything—it would be a real ordeal to show off in front of the girls. And, of course, she couldn't possibly be in the concert! She would be scared out of her life!

Mirabel saw her hesitate, and she went on pressing her. 'Gladys! Come on—be a sport. Look—if you'll show what you can do, and get the girls to put you into the concert, *I'll* write to your mother myself and tell her how well you did. See? Because I know you'll do well. And then think how pleased she'll be!'

The thought of Mirabel actually writing to her mother for her touched Gladys more than anything else could have done. She stared at Mirabel's earnest face, and tried to blink the tears that came far too easily.

'You are a good sort,' she said, rather chokily. 'You really are. I thought at first you were such a selfish, cold-hearted sort of girl—but you're not. Be friends with me, Mirabel. You haven't any friend here and neither have I. I'll do anything you ask me, if you'll be friends.'

'Well,' said Mirabel, remembering that it was the half-term the following week, 'I'm leaving soon, you know—at half-term. I never meant to stay longer than that. So it's not much use your being friends with me really—because I'll soon be gone.'

'Oh,' said Gladys, turning away. 'That's just my luck. People I like always go away.'

'Now don't start that sort of thing again,' said Mirabel, half-impatiently. 'All right. I'll be your friend till I go—but mind, you've got to be sensible and do what I say. And the first thing I say is—you've got to show the girls how you can act!'

It was quite pleasant to have some one taking such an interest in her! Gladys felt warmed, and looked gratefully at Mirabel. She was a weak, timid character—Mirabel was strong and decided, even though she was often wrong.

'Yes—I will show the girls if you want me to,' Gladys said.

'Well, after tea, in the common room this evening, you show them,' said Mirabel. 'I'll clap like anything at the end, so you needn't be afraid. Perhaps the girls will put you in the concert after all, when they see how good you are. Isabel said something about not being able to alter the programmes—but I'm sure it could be done. I could help.'

Mirabel felt rather proud of having got her own way with Gladys. She told Hilary and the others, and they looked forward with interest to seeing what Gladys could do that evening.

It certainly was a surprise to everyone! Gladys looked terribly nervous at first, and her voice shook. But in a minute or two, as she forgot herself, and threw herself heart and soul into the part she was acting, it seemed as if the little Misery-girl was no longer there—but some one quite different, that nobody had seen before!

Gladys acted many parts from different Shakespeare plays—Lady Macbeth—Miranda—Malvolio—Hamlet. She knew them all by heart. Her mother had been very fond of Shakespeare's works and the two of them had studied them together evening after evening. Gladys' dead father had been a fine actor, and Gladys had inherited the gift.

Gladys stopped at last, changing from Bottom the Weaver to her own timid self. The girls roared with delight at her, and clapped loudly.

'You monkey! Fancy not telling us you could do all that!' said Pat. 'You'll bring the house down at the concert! I say—we simply MUST put her in! Can't we possibly?'

'Please, please don't,' begged Gladys in alarm. 'I couldn't possibly do it in front of most of the school. Well, I might, if I'd more time to rehearse with you. But the concert's tomorrow. I should die if you made me be in it! Please don't!'

'Well—if you feel so strongly about it, I suppose we'll have to leave you out,' said Janet. 'Is there, by any chance, anything else you've kept us in the dark about? Can you paint marvellous pictures—or work wonderful sums in your head?'

Gladys laughed—the first laugh since she had been at St. Clare's. 'There's only one other thing I'm good at,' she said. 'That's lacrosse.'

'Well, you don't seem to have shone there to any great extent,' said Bobby, in surprise.

'I know. I didn't bother,' said Gladys. 'I just didn't care whether I ran fast or not, or scored a goal, or anything. That's why Miss Wilton kept making me goalkeeper, I expect. She thought I was only good for stopping goals, not for anything else. But I *can* play well, if

I try. I was in the top team at my day school.'

'Good,' said Mirabel. 'We'll make you shoot dozens of goals and then you can write that to your mother, too.'

'Sorry about your mother, Gladys,' said Hilary. 'Tell us any news you get. We're all interested.'

Gladys went to bed really happy that night. She had a friend. She had been clapped and applauded. She had thrown off her reserve, and let the other girls speak to her of her mother. Things didn't seem so bad now. For the first time she fell asleep without lying and worrying.

In the middle of the night, five of the girls lay and tossed restlessly. Pat and Isabel, Doris, Bobby and Carlotta could not sleep. Their throats hurt them. They coughed and sneezed. It was most annoying—because the concert was to be the next evening!

'I shan't be able to speak a word,' thought Doris, as she tried to ease her throat. 'This really is bad luck. I can't possibly be in the concert. Blow! I was so looking forward to it.'

In the morning all five went along to Matron, feeling very miserable and sorry for themselves. She took their temperatures.

'You've got the horrid cold that has been running round the school,' she said, briskly. 'You've all got temperatures except Carlotta—and it would take a lot to give *her* one! But she can go to bed just the same. To the san, all of you.'

'But Matron—it's the concert tonight!' said Bobby, hoarsely. 'We can't possibly go to bed.'

'Put your coats on and your hats and scarves,' said Matron, taking no notice of Bobby at all. 'And go across to the san, immediately. You've all got the same feverish cold, that's plain—caught the chill watching lacrosse in that cold wind the other day, I suppose—so the germ found you easy prey. Bobby, are you deaf? Go and get your coat and hat at once and don't stand arguing.'

It never was any good trying to argue with Matron. She had dealt with girls for many, many years, and bed and warmth and the right medicine in her opinion cured most things very quickly. So, concert or no concert, the five girls were bundled into bed in the san, and there they lay, moaning about the concert and wondering what was going to happen.

It didn't take the rest of the form long to decide what was to happen.

'We can't *possibly* hold the concert without those five!' said Hilary.

'Doris was one of the stars,' said Janet.

'*And* Bobby,' said Hilary. 'And Carlotta too. It would be a very weak affair without those three. We'll have to postpone it. We'll have it next week.'

'We can't,' said Anna. 'The third form are having theirs.'

'Well, the week after,' said Hilary. 'That will give the invalids time to get over their colds. I hope nobody else feels like sneezing or coughing! If they do, for goodness' sake go to the san, and get it over, so that we can have the concert all right in a fortnight's time !'

'Gladys can be in it this time !' said Katheleen. 'That makes another good performer.'

'Oh, good!' said Anna, looking at Gladys. 'That will be fine. You'll have loads of time to practise and rehearse now, Gladys.'

Gladys couldn't help feeling thrilled. She did love acting—and it would be fun to rehearse with the others. It hadn't been nice to be left out. Now she would be able to join in, and would be clapped just as the others were. There would be a lot to tell her mother when she wrote. She felt

a wave of gratitude welling up for Mirabel. It was Mirabel
who had made all this possible for her.

She went up to Mirabel and slipped her arm through
hers. 'It's a pity about the others, isn't it?' she said. 'But
they'll be better in a fortnight—and I *shall* like being in the
concert now. I shall clap like anything when your turn
comes, Mirabel. I think you'll be the best of us all.'

Mirabel did not smile. She looked rather cold and blank.
Gladys wondered what the matter was.

'How many pieces are you going to play?' she asked.
'Do you want me to turn over the pages for you at the
piano?'

'I shan't *be* in the concert,' said Mirabel, in a funny,
even voice. 'You know I'm going home at half-term—and
by the time the concert comes, I'll be gone. I feel disappointed, of course—so don't keep on rubbing it in!'

She took her arm from Gladys's and walked off. How
sickening everything was!

12   GLADYS TACKLES MIRABEL

THE second form seemed to have dwindled considerably
now that five of them were away. Hilary and Alison went
down with the cold the next day, so there were many empty
desks. The concert was put off for two weeks, and the
second form girls felt very flat and gloomy.

Elsie was the only one who was at all pleased. She had

consistently refused to take any interest at all in the concert, and she felt glad that this disappointment had come upon the others. As Anna had predicted, Elsie had adopted a martyr—like attitude, looking left-out and miserable all day long. But no one took the slightest notice of her.

The girl's pride was hurt. She had not liked to ask Anna what she had said to Miss Theobald on the day when both of them had been sent for. But it was clear to her now, that not only the girls no longer regarded her as one of their heads, but Miss Jenks also appeared to think that only Anna was head-girl. It was most exasperating. Elsie sometimes wished she was like Carlotta and could slap and box people's ears when she felt like it! She would box the ears of every one in the form!

The seven girls in the san had a bad time for the first day or two, and then, when their temperatures went down, they sat up and recovered their spirits. It was fun for so many to be together. They could play games and talk.

'It's half-term next week,' said Isabel. 'Our mother's coming over to take us out.'

'So's mine,' said Doris. 'Carlotta, is your father coming to take you out?'

'Yes—and my grandmother too,' said Carlotta, gloomily. 'I get on with my father all right now—but I just seem to go all common and bad-mannered with my grandmother. I remember all my circus ways, and she just hates them. Oh dear—I meant to try and get terribly good-mannered this term, and not box any one's ears or lose my temper or anything.'

Mirabel is supposed to be going at half-term, isn't she?' said Bobby, suddenly. 'She won't be in the concert then —and she won't know if she's been chosen to play in any of the lacrosse matches, either—and she'll miss the birthday feast that Carlotta's going to give.'

'She's an idiot,' said Doris. 'She can't think straight.

That's what's the matter with her.'

'She wouldn't be a bad sort if she made up her mind to shake down and be sensible,' said Pat. 'I quite like her now. And I must say she's good to that timid little Gladys. When Katheleen came in to see us yesterday, she said that Mirabel really does look after her and walk with her—and Gladys is like a little dog with her—trots after her and does everything she's told.'

'Well, who would have thought that those two would pair up!' said Isabel. 'And there's another astonishing thing too—who would have thought that lazy old Anna would pull herself together as she has done!'

By that week-end the seven invalids were very much better. They could not possibly have attended the concert, if theirs had been postponed only a week, so it was just as well that it had been put off for three weeks. They would be well enough to go to the third form's concert, which was on the Thursday before half-term.

Mirabel was looking very glum. Half-term seemed to be coming quickly. The postponing of the concert had been a bitter disappointment. It was dull without half the class at lessons.

The only bright spot was her new friendship with Gladys. The girl was showing unsuspected sides of her character to Mirabel. She could make excellent jokes, and had a fine sense of humour. She was fun to walk with because she could keep up a merry chatter. She seemed to have quite thrown off her pre-occupation with her own troubles. She really was very fond of Mirabel, and the girl, although embarrassed at any show of affection in the ordinary way, liked to feel Gladys slipping her arm through hers.

'Mirabel! You won't really go home at half-term, will you?' Gladys said that week-end. 'There are only a few days more. It's lovely being friends with you. Don't go, will you?'

'Of course I'm going,' said Mirabel, impatiently. 'I told you I'd made up my mind to go at half-term, even before I arrived here! And I'm not going back on that. I never go back on what I've said.'

'No. I know you don't,' said Gladys, with a sigh. 'It's only people like me who change their minds and alter what they meant to do. But I do wish you weren't going, Mirabel.'

Gladys said the same thing to Hilary that day, when she went to see her in the san. 'I do so wish Mirabel wasn't going,' she said. 'I feel a different person since she was nice to me, and all of you clapped me that time I acted for you.'

'What's she got to go for?' said Hilary. 'She has settled down all right. She's happy. She's one of us now, and she enjoys life here. Whatever does she want to go home at half-term for, now she's all right?'

'Well, you see,' said Gladys, earnestly, 'she can't go back on what she said. She *said* she was going home at half-term—she made up her mind about that—so she can't *possibly* change her mind, can she? She's such a strong character, you see.'

'Well, it is strong characters who ought to be able to change their minds at times,' said Hilary. 'I call it weak to stick to something when you know it's silly. And it is silly for Mirabel to go back home now. We want her for the concert. She knows that she's just being weak, not strong!'

Gladys was astonished to hear this. It seemed to make things quite different. Weak little Gladys had thought that strong characters must be able to make right decisions and carry them out—but now she saw that a strong character could do something quite new to her. She stared at Hilary.

'I wish you'd say that to Mirabel,' she said.

'Say it yourself,' said Hilary. 'You're her friend, aren't you? Well, *you* tell her!'

'She wouldn't listen to *me*,' said Gladys.

'What you mean is—you're afraid to tackle her!' said Hilary, with a laugh. 'Go on, mouse—take the bull by the horns—and if you really do care for Mirabel and want her for your friend, don't be afraid of telling her what you think. Get a little spunk!'

Poor Gladys! Every one always seemed to be telling her to get a little 'spunk.' It was something she was sure she would never possess. She had been such a mother's girl that now it was difficult for her to stand on her own feet.

'All the same—it's no good having a friend unless you'll do something for them,' thought Gladys, trying to screw up her courage. 'I shall lose Mirabel if I don't tackle her—and if I lose her because she's angry with me for tackling her, well, I shan't be any worse off. So I'll do it.'

It wasn't easy. It never is easy for a timid person to tackle a strong one, especially if it is to point out that the strong one is wrong. Gladys went to Mirabel and slipped her arm through hers.

'Mirabel,' she said, 'I've been thinking over what you said about going home—and not changing your mind and all that—and I really do think you're wrong.'

'That's my own business,' said Mirabel, rather roughly.

'No, it isn't. It's mine too,' said Gladys, hoping her voice would not begin to tremble. 'You're my friend, and I don't want you to go.'

'I've told you I can't change my mind. I never do,' said Mirabel. 'Don't bother me.'

'If you were really as strong a character as you make out, you *would* change your mind,' said Gladys, boldly. 'You know you could stay here happily now—but you're too proud to own you've been silly—and you call it being strong enough not to change your mind!'

'Gladys! How *dare* you talk to me like this!' cried Mirabel, astonished and angry. 'Anybody would think you are Miss Theobald—picking me to pieces—telling me I'm no good—not worth-while!'

'I'm not telling you that,' said Gladys, getting distressed. 'I'm only saying—don't let your pride stand in the way of your happiness. That's all.'

Mirabel wrenched her arm out of Gladys's and walked off, red in the face. How dare Gladys say things like that to her? She put on her hat and coat and went out into the school grounds, fuming.

Gladys stared after her, miserable. 'I knew it wouldn't be any good,' she thought. 'Of course Mirabel wouldn't let me say things like that. Now she won't even be friends with me for the last two or three days before she goes!'

Mirabel walked round the grounds, hot and angry. But, as her anger died, her mind began to work more calmly. There was a great deal in what Gladys had said. 'Though how that timid little thing ever thought that all out beats me!' said Mirabel to herself. 'There must be more in her than I thought. And the way she stood up to me too! She *has* come on. She must like me a lot to make up her mind to go for me like that, in order to try and make me change my mind, so that she can still have me for a friend.'

The wind cooled her hot cheeks. She sat on the wall and looked down over the valley. It was very pleasant there. It would be marvellous in the summer. St. Clare's *was* fun—there was no doubt about that.

'Now, let's think things out calmly,' said Mirabel to herself. 'I was angry because my family sent me away because I didn't fit in at home—and I vowed to get back as soon as I could just to show them they couldn't send me away! Now I like being here-and I see that I am better

"How dare Gladys say anything like that to me,"
thought Mirabel

away from home, and shall go back really thrilled to see every one. I dare say I'll learn lots of things here I ought to have learnt before—thinking of other people, not always having my own way and things like that. Well then-what is stopping me from staying here?'

She gazed down on the valley, and did not like to think out the answer. But she had to.

'All that is stopping me is, as Gladys pointed out, my pride. I'm too proud to tell Daddy that I'll stay. I was so angry at being sent away that I wanted to pay them out by coming back as soon as possible and being beastly. And I think I'm a strong character! Golly, all this makes me sound as hateful as catty Elsie!'

She stayed for a few minutes longer and then she sprang down from the wall. She went into the school building and took off her out-door things. She went straight to Miss Theobald's room and knocked at the door.

'Come in!' said Miss Theobald. She was talking to Miss Jenks and Mam'zelle. Mirabel was a little taken aback when she saw all three teachers there—but what she had come to say had to be said, no matter how many people were in the room.

'Miss Theobald,' she said, rather loudly. 'May I stay on, please, and not go home at the half-term? Would you let me? I like being here, and I'm sorry I was so silly at first.'

Miss Theobald looked at the girl, and smiled her nicest smile, warm and friendly.

'Yes—we shall be very glad to have you,' she said. 'Isn't that so, Miss Jenks—Mam'zelle?'

'It is,' said Miss Jenks and nodded kindly at Mirabel.

'Ha!' said Mam'zelle, 'c'est bien, cal! I too am pleased.'

'I will telephone to your parents,' said Miss Theobald. 'I am glad, Mirabel, that you have something "worth-while" in you—no, I don't mean your music! Something better than that. Well done!"

Praise like this was very sweet. Mirabel walked out of the room, warm and happy. She knew she had a great deal to learn—things would go wrong, and she would make mistakes—but nothing could take that moment from her.

She went to find Gladys. She found her curled up in a corner of the common room, looking rather small and woe-begone. She went over to her and gave her an unexpected hug.

'Well, old thing! I'm staying on! I've just been to tell Miss Theobald. And all because you ticked me off like that, and set me thinking!'

Half in tears Gladys returned the hug. It was marvellous. She, a weak person, had summoned up enough strength to tackle a strong one-and had actually got what she wanted. It was too good to be true.

'You'll be in the concert!' she said. 'And you'll come to Carlotta's feast. What fun we'll have! Oh Mirabel I'm so proud of you!'

'I'm rather proud of you too,' said Mirabel, awkwardly. 'You gave me a surprise, telling me home-truths like that. You're a good sort of friend to have.'

'What a lot I shall have to write and tell my mother!' said Gladys. 'And I say—won't every one be pleased you've changed your mind and are staying on!'

The girls *were* pleased. They had begun to like Mirabel now, and they admired her for being able to alter her mind and own that she had been wrong. Soon they would forget Mirabel's extraordinary behaviour the first few weeks of the term.

Only one girl was displeased. That was Elsie. Why should such a fuss be made of that ridiculous Mirabel who had behaved so badly, and who had been partly the cause of Elsie's disgrace? Elsie brooded over this and cast many spiteful glances at Mirabel, wondering what she could do to pay her out for being popular, when she, Elsie, was never taken any notice of at all!

But Mirabel was thick-skinned. She neither saw nor felt Elsie's hostility, but looked forward happily to the remainder of the term at St. Clare's.

13   HALF-TERM HOLIDAY

HALF-TERM came and went. It was a pleasant break for every one. Most parents came to take out the girls for some kind of treat, and those that lived near enough went home for a day or two. Alison's parents were away so she went out with the twins and their mother.

'Well, how are you all getting on this term?' asked Mrs. O'Sullivan. 'Working hard, I hope?'

But nobody said anything about work. The twins poured out their news about the concert, and about la-crosse, and how Carlotta was going to have a feast on her birthday. Alison talked of nothing but her beloved Miss Quentin.

'She's awfully clever,' said Alison. 'It's lovely learning Drama under her. She says I have the making of a good little actress.'

'Oh do shut up talking about Miss Quentin,' groaned Pat. 'Mummy, last term Alison was all over Sadie Greene, that American girl—who, by the way, has never even *written* to you, Alison! And this term it's Miss

Quentin! Isn't there any medicine or pill we can give Alison to stop her raving about people ?'

Alison had been very hurt that her 'best' friend, Sadie, had not taken the trouble to write to her at all. She thought it was mean of Pat to remind her of it.

'Well, Miss Quentin wouldn't be like that,' she said. 'I've made her promise to write to me every week in the holidays. She's loyal, I know. I think she's marvellous.'

'She's beautiful, she's wonderful, she's marvellous, she's magnificent,' said Isabel, with a grin. 'But the thing is—what does she think of *you*, Alison? Not much, I bet! You're always going about thinking somebody is wonderful—you never seem to imagine they might be bored with you.'

The idea of her beloved Miss Quentin being bored with her made Alison hot and angry. She glared at the twins. Mrs. O'Sullivan saw the look.

'Now, now,' she said, 'don't let's waste our precious time in quarrelling, please. I've no doubt Miss Quentin is a very admirable person and I'm sure Alison works hard in *her* class, at least, if she doesn't in anyone else's.'

Mirabel's father and mother came over to see her at half-term, and took her out to lunch, a theatre, and tea afterwards. Mirabel was intensely excited at the thought of seeing them. She forgot all about the temper in which she had been when she had parted from them. She forgot the horrid things she had said, and the threats she had made. She stood at the front door, eagerly waiting for them.

When they arrived, they were startled by some one who hurled herself at them, flung her arms round them, and exclaimed in a choky voice, 'Mummy! Daddy! It's lovely to see you again!'

Her mother and father looked at the excited girl, whose eyes shone with welcome. This was a different

Mirabel altogether! They hugged the girl, and looked with interest at the school. Neither of them had seen it. It had been a very sudden decision on Mirabel's father's part to send Mirabel away, and he had chosen a school recommended to him very highly by a friend. It had all been done in such a hurry that the parents had not had time to see the school itself.

'What a lovely place!' said Mrs. Unwin. 'Is there time to look round?'

'Mummy, you simply *must* see everything,' cried Mirabel, and she dragged her parents all over the school, from top to bottom, even showing them the bathroom where she had her nightly bath. There was great pride in the girl's voice. It was quite plain to them that Mirabel was extremely proud of St. Clare's already, and felt it to be her own splendid school.

'Daddy, I'm so pleased you chose St. Clare's,' said Mirabel, when they came back to the front door at last. 'It's marvellous. It really is.' She looked at her parents and hesitated a little. She had something to say that was difficult. Mirabel hated saying she was sorry about anything.

'You know—I really am sorry I was so awful at home,' said the girl, rushing her words out. 'I can see you all better now, because I'm far away from you—and I think I was awful to every one.'

'We've forgotten it all,' said her father. 'We shall never remember it again. All that matters to us is that you are happy—and will be happy when you come home again. We felt so proud when Miss Theobald let us know that you wanted to stay on. She said one or two nice things about you.'

'Did she really?' asked Mirabel, pleased. 'I hated her at first—she said some awful things to me—but now I think she's fine. Oh Mummy—I do wish you'd brought Joan and

Harry with you! I did want to see them.'

'They wanted to see you too,' said her mother. 'But it was too far to bring them. Now—what about going? We shall never get any lunch if we don't start soon.'

'Mummy-would you do something for me ?' asked Mirabel, suddenly. 'I've got a friend here-and her mother's ill in hospital, so there's no one to take her out for a half-term treat. Could she possibly come with us, do you think?'

'Of course,' said Mrs. Unwin, surprised and pleased to think that her difficult daughter had actually made a friend. She wondered what the friend would be like. She had never liked Mirabel's chosen friends before—they had always been noisy, impolite and out-of-hand—a little like Mirabel herself.

'I'll go and get her,' said Mirabel. She ran off to find Gladys. She was getting ready for the school lunch, feeling a little lonely, for nearly all the other girls had left for the half-term holiday.

Mirabel rushed at her. 'Gladys! You're to come with me! Go and ask Miss Jenks if you can come, quickly! Mummy and Daddy say you can come.'

A shock of joy ran through Gladys. She felt nervous of meeting Mirabel's parents—but to think that Mirabel wanted her to come was marvellous. Her depression fell away from her at once, and she stared in joy at her friend. She had few treats in her life, and it did seem to her that going out to lunch and a theatre was too good to be true.

'Gladys, don't stand staring there!' cried Mirabel, impatiently. 'Hurry up. Go and find Miss Jenks. I'll get your out-door things.'

In three minutes Gladys was at the front door with Mirabel, red with shyness, hardly able to say a word. Mr. and Mrs. Unwin took a look at the nervous girl, and were astonished. So this was Mirabel's friend—well, what

a change from the tiresome girls she had chosen before!
They took a liking to Gladys immediately, and Mrs. Unwin
smiled a motherly smile at her.

In some ways Mrs. Unwin resembled Gladys's own
mother. Both were the gentle, kindly type, and Gladys
warmed to Mrs. Unwin at once. In no time at all she
was telling Mrs. Unwin all about her own mother, rev-
elling in the understanding and kindness of Mirabel's
mother.

'I say! I do think you've got a nice mother!' she
whispered to Mirabel, when they went to wash their
hands at the hotel, before lunch. 'Next to mine, she's
the nicest I've ever met. And isn't your father jolly? I
feel a bit afraid of him but I do like him. Aren't you
lucky?'

Mirabel was pleased. She was seeing her mother and
father with different eyes, now that she had been away from
them for some weeks. It was pleasant to hear some one
liking them so much. She squeezed her friend's arm.

'It's fun having you,' she said. 'I'm glad my people like
you.'

A real surprise was in store for Gladys. When Mrs.
Unwin asked her what hospital her mother was in, she
heard Gladys's answer with astonishment.

'Why—that's quite near where my sister lives. I often
go over to see my sister—and perhaps I could go to the
hospital and find out how your mother is. I might even see
her, if she is allowed visitors.'

Gladys stared at Mrs. Unwin, red with delight. It would
bring her mother much closer somehow, if she knew some
one was going to the very hospital where her mother was.
And just suppose she was allowed to see her! Mrs. Unwin
could write and tell her about it.

'Oh thank you,' said the girl. 'If you only could! It would
be marvellous!'

The half-term went all too quickly. All the girls enjoyed it. It was a very pleasant break indeed, and they went back to school full of chatter about what they had done.

'Hallo!' said the twins, meeting Carlotta when they arrived back. 'How did you get on? Was your grandmother very stand-offish?'

'No—she seemed quite pleased with me,' said Carlotta, grinning. 'I didn't walk on my hands or do anything she disapproves of—and I made my hair so tidy you wouldn't know me. I was most frightfully polite to her, and my father was awfully pleased with me. He gave me a pound note for my birthday!'

'Gracious!' said Pat. 'What luck!'

'And my grandmother told me I could order anything I liked for my birthday party, at the shop in the town,' said Carlotta, her eyes lighting up with delighted expectancy. 'I say—won't we order lots of things! She gave me some things out of her store cupboard too. I've got a big box in the cupboard in our dormitory. I don't know what's in it yet, but I bet my grandmother has given me plenty.'

'How gorgeous!' said the twins. 'You sound as if you've got enough to feed the whole school.'

'No—just our form,' said Carlotta. 'And I'm not sure yet if we'll have it properly, in the afternoon at tea-time— or whether we'll make it really exciting, and go in for a midnight feast again. I think we ought to have a midnight feast every term, you know! School doesn't seem really complete without that!'

It looked as if the latter half of the term was going to be exciting. There was the concert to look forward to that week—several lacrosse matches—and now Carlotta's feast! All the girls glowed. What fun they had!

Bobby had a secret, and so had Janet. They had gone out together with Bobby's parents, and with Janet's brother, whose half-term holiday was the same week-end. He was as much of a monkey as Janet, always up to tricks. He had given Janet and Bobby an old trick to play on Mam'zelle. It was a curious looking thing, consisting of a long stretch of narrow rubber tubing, with a little bladder on one end, and an Indian rubber bulb on the other, which, when pressed, sent air down the tube into the little bladder, which at once expanded and became big.

'But what's it for?' asked the twins, in curiosity.

'You put the bladder under some one's plate at meal-time,' giggled Bobby, 'and run the tubing under the table-cloth. Then, when you press the bulb, the bladder fills and up tips the plate. Imagine Mam'zelle's astonishment when her plate starts dancing about! We shall all be in fits of laughter!'

This was really something to look forward to as well. Mam'zelle was a marvellous person to play tricks on. She was always taken in, and had caused more enjoyment than all the mistresses in the school put together.

'Oh Bobby! Let's do it soon,' begged Doris. 'Do let's. We haven't played any tricks this term, at all.'

'Well, after, all we *are* the second form,' said Janet, teasingly.

'Bobby will be playing tricks when she's head-girl!' said Isabel. 'I'm surprised she has gone as far as half-term without thinking of any.'

'Oh, I've *thought* of plenty,' said Bobby. 'But Miss Jenks isn't an easy person to play about with. She doesn't keep her temper like Miss Roberts did. She flares up suddenly, and I don't particularly want to be sent to Miss Theobald now I'm in the second form. It may have escaped your notice that I'm working hard this term! Don't forget I'm not Don't-Care Bobby as I was last term. I'm using my brains for other things besides tricks and jokes.'

'Let's have a rehearsal for the concert,' said Pat. 'We've

only got a few days now. Bring your violin, Mirabel—and Gladys, make up your mind what you're going to act, out of all the hundreds of parts you seem able to play. Come on, everybody—let's enjoy ourselves!'

14   A MARVELLOUS SHOW

THE days flew by, and the night of the concert came. Miss Jenks had to be lenient with the second form, because she could see that they really did mean their show to be a great success. Mam'zelle was the only teacher who would not make allowances, so the class groaned and worked for her as best they could.

'It is bad to have concerts in the middle of the term,' Mam'zelle grumbled to Miss Jenks. 'These girls, they think of anything but their work. Now, when I was a schoolgirl...'

'You worked all day and you worked all night, you had no games, you prepared no concerts...' chanted Miss Jenks, with her wide smile. The teachers had heard a thousand times of Mam'zelle's hard-worked youth.

'There are other things as important as lessons,' said Miss Roberts. 'We are not out to cram facts and knowledge into the girl's heads all day long, but to help them to form strong and kindly characters too. This concert now, that you grumble at—it is making the second form work together in a wonderful way, it is bringing out all kinds of unexpected talent—look at Mirabel and Gladys, for instance—and it will help a great cause. It makes the girls resourceful and ingenious too—you should see the costume Doris has made for herself as Matron and as cook.'

Mam'zelle did not know that Doris was going to imitate her as well. The other mistresses guessed it and they were looking forward to it. They all liked Mam'zelle, and admired her sense of humour. She could take a joke against herself very well.

'The third form concert was quite good,' said Miss Lewis, the history teacher. 'But I think the second form will be more entertaining. The third form were rather high-brow, and didn't provide a single laugh for any one. I fancy we shall find plenty to laugh at this Saturday!'

The second form were getting very excited. Only Elsie was apart from all the thrills and enjoyment. The girl still obstinately refused to take part in anything, and would not even be prompter.

'But Elsie, every one will think it very funny that you are the only second-former out of things,' said Pat, impatiently. 'We keep on offering you things to do, and you keep turning them down. I think it's very decent of us to be so patient with you.'

'I'll take part on one condition,' said Elsie, sullenly.

'What?' asked Bobby, coming up.

'That you let me be head-girl again with Anna,' said Elsie. 'You've punished me for weeks now, by taking away my authority as head-girl. Isn't it about time you let me have it back again?'

'Well—we'll ask the rest of the form,' said Pat. So that night in the common room, before a rehearsal was held, Anna put the question to the meeting.

'Elsie says she will take part in the concert if we let her be joint head-girl again. What does every one think about it?'

'Why should she bargain with us?' cried Carlotta. 'It is we who should bargain with her! We should say "You can be head-girl again if you show that you are worthy of it!"'

'Quite right,' called Doris.

'Look how she has behaved all these weeks,' said Janet. 'Has she tried to give us a better opinion of her? Has she shown us she could be trusted to lead us again? No—all she has done is to look spiteful, be catty when she has a chance, pose as a martyr and hope she'll get our sympathy. Well, she hasn't. We've just taken no notice at all, and she hasn't liked it.'

'I don't see why we should bother with her,' said Isabel. 'I really don't.'

'Will you show in the usual way whether you would like her again or not?' asked Anna. 'Hands up those who will give Elsie another chance as head-girl.'

Not a single hand went up. Anna grinned. 'Well,' she said, 'that's that. Elsie will have to put up with it. She hasn't come at all well out of this, I must say. I would have been willing to work with her again, if you'd said so—but I'm glad I haven't got to.'

Elsie was not there, and nobody bothered to fetch her to tell her what had happened. They began their rehearsal and were soon busy criticizing and applauding as one after another performed. Gladys was by now used to an audience and she acted as naturally as every one else. She and Doris were both natural actresses, though in a different way. Doris could imitate any one she had seen, but not act a part—and Gladys, quite unable to imitate any one around her, was excellent at interpreting any part in a play. The two admired each other and Gladys was fast making another friend.

'Well—I really think we've got everything all right now,' said Bobby at last. 'It *will* be fun ! Doris, you'll bring the house down with your imitation of Mam'zelle. I only hope Mam'zelle won't mind. But I don't think she will.'

The door opened and Elsie came in. 'You held the rehearsal without me,' she said. 'What do you want me to do at the concert?'

'Well, Elsie—you said you would only be in it if we recognized you as head-girl again,' said Anna, rather awkwardly. 'We put the question to the second form, and I'm afraid they decided not to give you the chance. So we didn't think you'd want to help with the concert, in that case.'

'Couldn't you have told me you wouldn't have me as head-girl, and still let me be in the concert?' said Elsie.

The others stared at her. 'Don't be silly,' said Bobby, at last. 'That's not the point. The point is, you always refused, and then wanted to make a bargain with us— and we wouldn't make it. I suppose you're beginning to feel very awkward about being left out of the concert in front of the whole school, so you're climbing down a bit, and want to help even if we won't accept you as head-girl again. Well—help if you like—but don't expect us to fall on your neck and give you a warm welcome, because we shan't.'

This was a long speech and Elsie listened to it in growing anger. All that Bobby said was true. Elsie was now beginning to feel horrified at being left out. Every one in the school would notice it. They would whisper about her. They would nudge one another as she passed. Elsie couldn't bear it. But neither had she the strength to overrule her rage and accept Bobby's luke-warm offer to let her help. She made a curious explosive noise of rage and walked out of the room.

Doris immediately imitated the explosive noise, and the whole form burst into laughter. Elsie heard the squeals, and stopped. She felt inclined to go back and hit out at every one. Then a wave of self pity overcame her and she burst into tears.

The concert was an enormous success. Half the school was there and all the mistresses. The curtain was drawn at exactly eight o'clock, and everything went like clock-work. The third form had been late in starting, and there had been long intervals between the various turns, which had bored the audience. But the second form were most efficient.

Turn after turn was put on and loudly applauded. Mirabel's playing was encored twice. The girl was so thrilled at her success that she could hardly speak for joy. Her piano-playing was really excellent, and as for her violin solo, it amazed every one, even the four music-teachers, who were by now used to gifted children springing up in their classes at times.

Carlotta's acrobatics were hailed with delight by the whole school. Every one knew that Carlotta had once been a circus-girl, and they clapped till their hands smarted when she did some of her graceful circus-tricks. The first-formers gaped in admiration and secretly determined to try out all the acrobatics themselves.

Gladys got an encore too. When the nervous, white-faced girl stepped on to the stage, the audience waited, rather critical, expecting to be bored. But before their eyes the girl changed into the characters she acted, and held the whole school spell-bound. She was really gifted, there was no doubt about it.

The most surprised person in the whole of the audience was Miss Quentin. She took the Drama class herself, and prided herself on knowing the capacities of everyone in the second form. Privately she had thought that Doris and Carlotta were the only ones worth teaching—and now here was the quiet little mouse, Gladys, bringing down the house with her polished and beautiful interpretations of many of the most difficult parts in Shakespeare's plays!

Miss Theobald leaned across to Miss Quentin. 'I must congratulate you on one of your pupil's performances!' she said, in her quiet voice. 'I can see that you must have helped the child a great deal. She could never have done all this by herself. It is amazing.'

Miss Quentin was not honest enough to say that she was as astonished as Miss Theobald. She loved praise as much as Alison did, and she nodded her head, pretending that she had taught Gladys all that she knew. Secretly she made up her mind to cultivate Gladys Hillman and give her the most important part in the play the second form were doing with her. She knew Alison had hoped for it—but she couldn't help that. Gladys must certainly have it. Then Miss Quentin could take all the credit to herself for the excellent performance she was sure Gladys would give!

The concert went on. The twins were applauded and so was Janet. The first-formers loved Bobby's conjuring tricks, and her ceaseless, ridiculous patter, and gave her an encore! But it was Doris who was the real star of the evening!

When she stepped on to the stage, dressed up as the jolly, fat old cook, there was a roar of delighted laughter. Doris pretended to make a pudding , keeping up a monologue in the cook's Irish accent, bringing in all the phrases that the girls knew so well. They squealed with laughter.

Then she altered her cook's uniform deftly—and lo and behold, there was Matron! Bobby ran on with some big bottles of medicine and a thermometer, and Doris proceeded to imitate Matron interviewing various girls sent to her for treatment of inspection.

Matron was in the audience, shaking with laughter. The girls roared with delight, missing many of Doris's jokes because they could not stop laughing. She was extremely clever and extremely funny.

'She should be on the stage,' said Matron, wiping her streaming eyes. 'Oh, am I really as funny as that? It's time I retired if I'm such a joke. This girl will be the death of me! Wait till she comes for medicine! I'll get my own back then!'

Doris went off the stage, grinning. The audience looked at the next item she was to do-another impersonation. Who?

They knew as soon as she appeared again. She had made herself plump with padding. She had scraped back her hair into a bun, put on enormous flat-heeled shoes, secretly borrowed from Mam'zelle's room, and wore glasses crookedly on her nose.

'Mam'zelle!' shrieked the girls, in delight. 'Marvellous!'

Doris approached the edge of the stage and addressed the girls in Mam'zelle's identical voice, taking off her English accent to perfection. The audience roared with laughter as Doris scolded them for misbehaviour.

'*C'est abominable!*' she finished. Then she turned away, re-arranged some things on a desk behind, and proceeded to take a lesson in the way that Mam'zelle took it, with hands wagging towards the ceiling, and her glasses slipping down over her nose.

Every one looked at Mam'zelle herself to see how she was taking it. Mam'zelle was lying back in her chair, helpless with laughter, tears pouring down her cheeks. The girls felt a warm wave of liking for her-how nice she was to laugh at some one taking off her little foibles and mannerisms! The girls had to laugh at Mam'zelle's squeals as much as at Doris's acting.

It was a marvellous show and a great success. Every one had loved it, and crowded round at the end to clap the performers on the back, and congratulate them. It was pleasant for both Mirabel and Gladys to feel these pats and hear the generous words of praise.

'Mother will hardly believe it all,' said Gladys to herself, her face shining with delight. 'I must tell her every single thing. And wasn't Mirabel's playing good? I clapped till my hands were sore.'

'We've made four pounds, three shillings and six-pence by selling tickets, programmes and getting in extra subscriptions,' announced Anna. 'Isn't that good? I bet no form will do as well as that.'

The second form enjoyed coffee and biscuits for a treat after the show, generously provided by Matron and Mam'zelle. 'Though why we should do this for a form whose chief success is putting up Mam'zelle and my-self to be laughed at, I really don't know !' said Ma-tron, beaming round. 'By the way—where's Elsie? She wasn't in the concert, and I don't see her now.'

The second form were so elated by their success that they wanted Elsie to join in the coffee and biscuits. But she was nowhere to be found.

She was in bed, alone—but not asleep; the only girl who had not shared in or applauded her form's success! Poor Elsie—her thoughts were very bitter that night, as she heard the echoes of laughter from the concert-room!

15   ELSIE IS FOOLISH

THE next big event was Carlotta's birthday. She was fifteen, and planned a really food feast. She had opened the box of goodies given to her by her grandmother, and it had proved to be even better than the second form had hoped.

'Sardines!' said Bobby, taking out three or four of the oblong tins. 'And what's this—an ENORMOUS tin of pine-apple chunks. It's ages since I've tasted pine-apple. And what a fine big tin!'

'Bars of chocolate-cream!' said Janet. 'Enough to feed the whole school, I should think!'

'Tins of prawns!' cried Hilary. 'I say—I do like prawns. Golly—prawns and pine-apple—what a heavenly mixture that would be!'

'Here's a ginger-bread cake,' said Alison. 'Isn't it big? Carlotta, I must say you own a first-class grandmother! Mine's good for a cake and a bottle of boiled sweets, but that's about all. Yours is super!'

'Well, she's only just begun to be super,' said Carlotta, with a grin. 'When she didn't approve of me, she handed me out two shillings and a new hair-slide. See what happens when she *does* approve of me!'

'Let's teach Carlotta some really marvellous manners,' said Janet, 'so that she will make a wonderful impression on her grandmother in the Christmas hols. She'll come back with half a grocer's shop then, I should think!'

'Oh, I say—what's this?' said Bobby, pulling out what looked like a large medicine bottle full of a yellow liquid. She read the label on it, then laughed.

"Sardines!" said Bobby, "and a huge tin of pineapple."

'Do listen. "One table-spoonful of this to be taken by each girl after the birthday feast!" Oh Carlotta, your grandmother is a scream.'

'Did you say you could go down to the tuck-shop in the town and order anything else you liked for your birthday?' asked Hilary, looking at the fine selection of things anything else, do you?'

'I'd like a good big birthday cake with fifteen candles on,' said Carlotta. 'I know candles are childish when you're fifteen, but I can't help it. I think a cake looks so pretty when they are all lighted. And, if we have the party at night, we can let the cake-candles light us !"

' Are we *really* going to have the feast at night?' asked Mirabel, thrilled. 'I've often read of midnight feasts in school-stories, but I didn't really think they happened.'

'Of course they happen!' said Bobby. 'You wait and see what we'll do.'

'I must order heaps and heaps of ginger-pop,' said Carlotta. 'I always feel I can drink a lot at night. And I'll get lemonade too. And buns we can butter and put jam on. I like those. It's a pity we can't cook kippers too. I do like kippers.'

Every one laughed. Carlotta loved kippers and pineapple, two things she had had a good deal of in her circus days. She had often described to the girls how lovely frying kippers smelt, being cooked on a stove in the open-air, in the dark of the night after a show.

'No, Carlotta—we must draw the line at kippers,' said Anna. 'The smell would wake the whole school. You know how we smell kippers frying even when Cook has the kitchen and the scullery door shut.'

Elsie heard all the talk about Carlotta's birthday. She knew there was to be a feast or a party of some sort. She saw the amount of goodies taken out of Carlotta's box, and she wondered if she was going to be asked or not.

The others debated the point when Elsie was not in the room.

'Are we going to ask Catty Elsie, or not?' said Pat.

'Not,' said almost every one.

'Oh, yes, let's,' said easy-going Anna. 'She likes good things as much as any one.'

'I daresay—but we don't want her spiteful face glowering at us all the time,' said Isabel.

At this moment Elsie came to the door of the common room. She stood outside, listening. She was always wondering if the others were discussing her. This time they were!

'Well, as it's my birthday and I can choose my own guests,' said Carlotta. 'It's for me to say whether I'll ask Catty Elsie or not.'

'Yes—all right—*you* say, Carlotta!' cried half a dozen voices at once.

'Well—I say this—I'll ask her, but at the same time I'll tell her she's got to drop this awful pose of being a miserable martyr and act sensibly,' said Carlotta. 'She goes about looking like a wet dish-cloth. I'm sure every one in the school must laugh at her. She's a disgrace to our form. Anyway, I'll ask her to the feast, and see if she's properly grateful and will behave herself.'

'Yes, do that,' said Anna, who was as tired as any one else to weep at any moment. 'Maybe she learnt her lesson when she was left out of the concert. Perhaps she will jump at the chance of being friends again.'

'Poor Catty Elsie,' said Doris, and she began to imitate Elsie's rather high, silly voice, tearful and excited. Every one roared with laughter.

They had no idea at all that Elsie was outside the door, listening. They would have been very scornful of her if they had known that, for eaves-dropping was not looked on favourably by any member of the second form. They had very strict ideas of honour and liked to keep to them.

Elsie forgot that those who listen behind doors seldom hear any good of themselves. She stood there, trembling with anger and self-pity, hating all the girls who tossed her name about so scornfully, had laughed at her so unkindly.

A movement towards the door made her hurry away quickly. She turned a corner and went into a cloak-room, pretending to fetch a pair of shoes. The second-formers, pouring out of their common room to go to a Nature meeting, did not guess that she had overheard nearly all they had said.

There was no time then to ask Elsie to the party, for the girls were already late for the meeting. Elsie joined them, and sat sulkily silent whilst the second and third-formers decided various matters concerning the Nature-Club. She didn't hear a word that was said. She remembered instead what she had just overheard, and looked with rage at Carlotta and the others. How she wished she could punish them in some way!

That night Carlotta went up to where Elsie was sewing in the common room. 'Elsie! I expect you know I'm having a birthday soon, don't you? '

'I should think the whole school knows,' said Elsie, spitefully.

'Well—I'm having a party or a feast of some kind,' said Carlotta. 'And every one is coming. The thing is—I'd like you to come too—but only if you'll pull yourself together and act sensibly. We're all tired of the way you're behaving. Come on, Elsie, now—can't you have a bit of common sense and be one of us? We don't like you a bit as you are now, but we are quite willing to change out ideas of you, if you'll be sensible.'

'Very kind of you, *very* kind of you indeed,' said

Elsie, in a trembling, sarcastic voice. 'The great Carlotta is most bountiful and condescending! And I know I should be very grateful and bow before her, thanking her for her great kindness!'

'Don't be an idiot,' said Carlotta, uncomfortably.

'I'm not,' said Elsie, changing her tone and voice and almost snarling at the surprised Carlotta. 'I'm just saying– – "No, thanks! *I'm* not coming to your beastly feast." Ho– –be a good little girl and you can come to the party! That's what you've said to me—me, who ought to be your head-girl! I would hate to come! And what is more, if you're going to hold it at night, Anna had better look out. You're second-formers now, not first-formers, and if you're caught, Anna will soon find *she* isn't head-girl any more, either.'

'You're impossible, Elsie,' said Carlotta, in disgust at Elsie's tone of voice. 'Well, if you don't want to come, don't. I for one am pleased.'

'So are we all!' cried Pat, Isabel and a few others, who had listened in indignation to Elsie's stinging speech. 'Keep away, Elsie. The party will be better without you!'

Elsie went on with her sewing, pursing up her thin lips scornfully. She badly wanted to go to the party, for she loved good things as much as anyone else. But her spite-fulness and obstinacy made it impossible for her to climb down and accept. She sat sewing thinking that if she could possibly prevent the party from being held, she would. 'If I could find out when and where Carlotta is going to hold it, I could drop a hint to Miss Jenks,' she thought. 'Miss Jenks doesn't look kindly on things like that. I've only got to say a word—or write an anonymous note—and the feast would be stopped before it had begun. That would be fine!'

But the others did not mean to let Elsie know when the feast was to be held! They felt certain she would try to spoil it in some way. They had decided to hold it on the

night of Carlotta's birthday, in the common room itself. If
they drew the blinds, and shut the door, they were reasonably safe. The common room was a good way away from
any Mistresses' room, and yet fairly near their own dormitories.

They talked about it with excitement whenever Elsie
was not in the room. As soon as she appeared they
dropped the subject at once. Not one girl, not even silly
little Alison, mentioned the subject when Elsie was there,
much as they sometimes wanted to.

Carlotta had been down to the shop in the town and
ordered what she wanted. The cake was to be a magnificent affair, with fifteen coloured candles. It was to have
pink icing, with roses round the edge, and silver balls and
sugared violets for decoration. The candles were to be
fixed in roses made of sugar. Every one was very excited
about it.

'The ginger-pop has come,' announced Carlotta, gleefully. 'I got the boy who brought it, to put it at the back
of the bicycle shed. I was afraid Miss Jenks would have
a fit if she saw all those bottles of ginger-beer and lemonade arriving for me. We'll each have to bring in a
bottle or two when it's safe,'

'It will be fun,' said Mirabel. She looked at Gladys,
who was beaming too. 'I'm glad I stayed on. Fancy
missing Carlotta's feast! I would have been an idiot.'

'You would,' said Gladys. The mouse-like girl was
no longer the Misery-girl. She laughed and smiled with
the rest, and followed Mirabel about like a shadow. The
bigger girl was very fond of her, and the two were quite
inseparable. St. Clare's had already done a good deal
for both of them!

'We'd better not cook anything at all,' said Pat. 'I
remember when we fried sausages once in the middle of
the night, they made a terrific smell. We'd better just be

content with cold things. We'll borrow some plates from the dining-room cupboard. There are heaps of old ones on the top shelves that won't be missed for a day or two.'

It was fun to plan everything—fun to smuggle glasses and mugs, plates and dishes and spoons and forks into the common room. Carlotta's birthday was coming nearer and nearer. The birthday cake was made and the girls went down to the shop to inspect it. It was marvellous.

'I wish your birthday night would come, Carlotta!' said Pat. 'What sport we'll have! And *what* a feast!'

16   CARLOTTA'S BIRTHDAY PARTY

THE girls were gathered in their common room, the day before Carlotta's birthday. Alison took a quick look round the room. Elsie was not there.

'What time's the feast tomorrow night?' she asked. 'Exactly at midnight? Let's make it *exactly*! It's much more thrilling. Miss Quentin calls it the "witching midnight hour", and somehow...'

'I suppose you'd like to ask your beloved Miss Quentin?' said Isabel, pulling Alison's curly hair. 'Can you see her sitting here in out common room, her hair done up in curl-papers, her face shining with grease, eating pine-apple chunks and sardines? I can't.'

'She *doesn't* do her hair in curl-papers,' and Alison, indignantly. 'She's got beautiful, naturally wavy hair. Why are you always so unkind about her? I wish she could come to the feast. I'm sure she'd love it.'

'Well, *we* shouldn't,' said Pat, who had no great liking for the rather affected teacher of Drama. 'You make me sick the way you go mooning round after Miss Quentin. She's not so marvellous as you think she is. I think it was pretty mean of her to take the credit to herself for Gladys's acting at out concert the other night.'

'Whatever do you mean?' cried Alison, indignantly.

'Well, Alison, you know when Gladys put up that grand performance of Shakespeare's characters the other night,' said Pat, who thought it was about time that Alison was cured of her senseless admiration for Miss Quentin.

'Yes,' said Alison.

'Well, at the end of it, Miss Theobald leaned across to Miss Quentin and congratulated her on Gladys's performance and said she was sure she herself had coached her for it,' said Pat, mercilessly. 'And your wonderful Miss Quentin just nodded and smiled and looked pleased —and didn't say that she knew nothing about Gladys Hillman's acting powers at all! We all think that was pretty mean.'

'I don't believe it!' cried Alison, quick to defend the mistress she so much admired.

'Well, Pam Boardman was sitting near, and she heard it all,' said Pat. 'She told us. So now just stop thinking Miss Quentin is the world's greatest wonder.'

Alison changed the subject quickly. It really hurt her to hear such things of Miss Quentin. She was always one to shut her ears to possibly unpleasant things.

'To come back to what I was saying,' she said, 'What time's the feast tomorrow night?'

'Well, as you so badly want it at exactly midnight, we'll have it then,' said Carlotta. 'I've got a dear little alarm clock I'll set for the time—and one of you in the other dormitory can stick it under your pillow so that it'll wake you without rousing every one in the building. I daren't put it under *my* pillow because Miss Catty Elsie sleeps near me and would wake too. We want to be sure she doesn't know the time.'

'All right then—midnight exactly, tomorrow night,' said Doris, in her clear voice.

At that moment the door opened, and Hilary came in. She had been to the school library to choose a book. She looked round at the others.

'I hope you haven't been talking about anything that matters,' she said, ' because dear sweet-natured, honest-souled Elsie was outside the door, listening for all she was worth!'

The others stared at her in dismay.

'Blow!' said Carlotta. 'We *have* been talking about the feast—and we said a good many times it was to be midnight tomorrow. Blow, blow, blow!'

'Well, Elsie will certainly do her best to spoil it for us tomorrow night,' said Pat. 'She's sure to split on us somehow—absolutely sure to.'

'I'm not *going* to have our feast spoilt.' said Carlotta, in a determined voice. 'Pat, go to the door and see if Elsie's anywhere about now. Stay by the door and warn us if she comes.'

Pat looked outside the door. There was no one there. Elsie had got the information she wanted, and was content!

'Now listen,' said Carlotta, 'the feast is off for tomorrow night—but it's ON for tonight instead!'

'Goody, goody!' said every one, pleased.

'We must make sure Elsie doesn't hear us creeping out of the room,' said Bobby.

'She sleeps very soundly,' said Carlotta. 'I think we can manage it all right. Now, not a word, any one! We'll hold the feast tonight—and Elsie it's all over, and she hasn't been able to spoil it!'

Elsie had no idea that the time of the feast was altered. She hugged her secret all day long, pondering how she could spoil the feast without any one guessing it was she who had done so.

Should she tell Miss Jenks? That would certainly stop the feast, but Miss Jenks did not like tale-bearers. Should she write a note to Miss Jenks, informing her of the feast, but not sign her name? This seemed quite a good-idea—but then Miss Jenks might throw the note into the fire and take no notice of it. Elsie had once heard her say that no one should ever take notice of anonymous letters—they were too despicable even to read.

'It's no good writing a note that Miss Jenks won't read or take notice of,' thought the girl. 'I wish I knew the best way to spoil the feast.'

She thought about it earnestly—so earnestly that Mam'zelle nearly 'went up in smoke', as Bobby put it, because Elsie paid so little attention in the French class.

'Elsie! This is the third time I have asked you to come out and write on the blackboard,' said Mam'zelle, exasperated. 'Ah, I have the patience of a donkey or I would not put up with you.'

'You mean the "patience of an *ox*," Mam'zelle,' chuckled Bobby.

'A donkey is patient too,' said Mam'zelle. 'I need the patience of cows, donkeys, sheep and oxen too, when I deal with such a person as this Elsie. You will either depart from this room, Elsie, or pay attention to what I say. I will not have inattention in my class.'

Elsie had to give her thoughts to the French lesson after that—but during prep. time that evening she suddenly made up her mind what she would do.

'I'll wait till they're all out of the room tomorrow night —then I'll slip along to Miss Jenks's room and say I'm very worried because all the others have vanished,' thought

Elsie. 'She'll come back to see—and will then go and hunt around, and find every one feasting in the common room. I can say I am afraid they've been kidnapped or something. After all, that American girl, Sadie, was nearly kidnapped last term—so I can pretend to be afraid it's happened again!'

This seemed to Elsie a good idea. If she really pretended to be frightened that the others had been kid-napped, Miss Jenks would not think she was telling tales-and the others would not know she had given them away, because it would be Miss Jenks who suddenly came along and found them!

Elsie had no idea that the feast was for that night not the next. The second-formers kept their secret well. In fact, Carlotta and Bobby went a bit further, and whispered loudly together, in Elsie's hearing, about all that was to happen the night following! Elsie took it all in, and grinned to herself. Just wait, you second-formers, and see what happens to your wonderful feast tomorrow night!

That night Carlotta wound up and set her tiny alarm clock. She gave it to Katheleen, who slept in the next room with the others. 'Put it under your pillow,' she said. 'When it goes off, wake the others quietly. Then come and wake me in the next dormitory. I'll wake our lot and we'll all go to the common room as quiet as mice.'

Katheleen put the clock under her pillow. She felt sure she would not need it, because she was too excited to sleep. But sleep overtook one tired girl after another, and soon both dormitories were peacefully dreaming.

Elsie was fast asleep too. She was a heavy sleeper, and sometimes snored. Tonight she was huddled up beneath her blankets, because it was cold. She meant to sleep well that night so that she would be well-rested, and able to keep awake the following night.

Every one was asleep at midnight. The alarm clock under Katheleen's pillow suddenly went off with a tiny ringing noise. Katheleen woke with a jump. She put her hand under the pillow and stopped the alarm from ringing. No one else had waked up. Katheleen sat up in bed, hugging herself in joy. The midnight feast was about to begin!

She sprang out of bed and put on her slippers and dressing-gown. Then she went softly from one bed to another, shaking the sleepers, and whispering the magic word into their ears; 'Midnight feast! Midnight feast!'

Every one sat up at once. Dressing-gowns and slippers were groped for in the dark. Excited whispering rose.

'I can't find my slippers!'

'Blow this dressing-gown! The girdle's all tied in a knot!'

'Sh!' warned Katheleen. 'We've got to be careful not to wake dear Elsie, you know.'

She slipped into the next dormitory and made her way quietly to Carlotta's bed. Carlotta was under sheets and blankets, curled up like a little animal. Katheleen shook her gently. Carlotta shot upright in bed and Katheleen pressed her shoulder warningly.

'Midnight,' she whispered in Carlotta's ear. Carlotta's heart jumped for joy. Her birthday feast, of course! She padded round the dormitory as quietly as a cat, waking every one but Elsie.

There was no whispering in that room, and not a single giggle! Each girl took slippers and dressing-gown and crept quietly to the door. Elsie snored a little, much to every one's relief. Carlotta shut the door quietly—and locked it! She took out the key, and put it into her dressing-gown pocket. Now, if Elsie did wake up, she couldn't get out and spoil the feast!

Everyone went to the common room. Not until the door was fast-shut and cushions put along the bottom to hide the crack of light, was the light switched on. Then what a whispering and giggling there was!

'Elsie snored as we went out!' giggled Carlotta. 'Such a nice, gentle little snore! Now—come on—set out the plates and things!'

Everything was taken from the hiding-places—from the bottom of cupboards, and the back of shelves, from tuck-boxes and tins, and from behind books in book-cases. Soon the common room tables were set with the empty plates and dishes. The largest plate of all was put in the middle. That was for the lovely birthday cake.

'Now for a real, proper Feast!' said Carlotta, happily. She and the others set out the goodies they had-the cakes and the buns, the biscuits and the sweets. They opened the tins and emptied the contents on to dishes-sardines, fruit salad, pine-apple, prawns—the most wonderful selection of things imaginable!

Carlotta opened a dozen ginger-beer bottles. At each pop there was a giggle.

'Here's to our dear, sleeping-beauty, Elsie!' said Bobby, with a laugh, and drank the fizzy ginger-beer.

'Come-on, every one—let's really enjoy ourselves!'

17   THE SECOND FORM PLAY
A TRICK

THE second-formers certainly *did* enjoy themselves. After a bit they forgot to whisper, and began to speak in their normal voices. It didn't matter, really. They were too far from any sleeping mistress to be heard. They giggled at everything, and laughed till the tears came at Doris and her idiotic antics with empty ginger-beer bottles.

They ate everything. Carlotta even ate sardines and pineapple together. Alison tried prawns dipped in ginger-beer, which Pat and Isabel said were 'simply super', but they made her feel sick taken that way. However, the others didn't mind, and mixed all the food together with surprising results.

'Nobody would dream that sardines pressed into ginger-bread cake would taste so nice,' said Janet. 'My brother told me that and I didn't believe him. But it's true.'

The birthday cake was marvellous. It melted in the mouth! The candles were lighted very soon and the light turned off. All the girls sat munching happily, watching the fifteen candles flicker and glow. It was lovely.

'A happy year to you, Carlotta!' said Pat, holding up her mug of ginger-beer. 'It's your birthday now, because it's past midnight. Many happy returns of the day!'

'Thanks,' said Carlotta, her vivid little face radiant. Her dark eyes sparkled as she looked round at her friends. It was lovely to give people pleasure. She would tell her grandmother all about it.

'Happy returns!' said one voice after another. 'Happy

birthday! Good old Carlotta!'

Carlotta cut second slices of her big birthday cake for every one. There was a fairly big piece left, enough for two extra slices.

'Two more bits,' said Carlotta, slicing the piece in half. 'Who shall we give them to?'

'One to Miss Jenks!' said Pat. 'You needn't say we had the cake at midnight!'

'And one to Miss Quentin,' said Alison eagerly.

'Don't be silly,' said Carlotta. 'Do you think I'm going to waste my birthday cake on Miss Quentin! I'd rather give a slice to Elsie!'

'Well, let's,' said Anna, unexpectedly. 'It's supposed to be good for people to heap coals of fire on their head-you know, return good for evil—and anyway, what a shock for Elsie when we give a bit—and she realizes we've had the party!'

'We'll give it to her after the next night then,' said Carlotta, grinning. 'Let her try and spoil the feast this coming night—and then the next day we'll present her with a bit of cake. That really would be funny.'

Everyone agreed to that—not that they wanted to make Elsie a present at all—they just wanted to see her face when she saw the piece of cake, and realised that the feast had been held in peace without her, and hadn't been spoilt.

'Well, one bit for Miss Jenks, and the other for darling Elsie,' said Carlotta, and put them away in a tin. 'Now, girls, is there anything else left to eat?'

There wasn't—and very little to drink either. 'It's a good thing,' said Anna. 'I simply couldn't eat another crumb!'

'Fancy *you* saying that, Anna!' said Pat, with a laugh, looking at the plump, round-faced girl. 'I should have thought you could have gone on eating till breakfast-time!'

'Don't be rude to your head-girl,' said Anna, lazily.

Nothing ever ruffled her good temper. 'Carlotta, we'd better clear up and get back. We've been here ages!'

'What a pity!' said Alison, with a sigh. She never liked clearing up. The girls set to work and stacked the dishes and plates neatly at the back of a cupboard, hoping they would be able to wash them and put them back into their proper places in the morning.

They swept up the crumbs and threw them out of the window. They put the ginger-beer and lemonade bottles into a cupboard outside in the passage. Then they looked round the common room. There was not a single sign of the lovely feast they had had.

'Good girls,' said Anna. 'Now come along—as quietly as you can, so as not to wake Elsie.'

The second-formers crept quietly back to their rooms. Carlotta unlocked her dormitory door. The first sound that greeted her was the light snoring of the sleeping Elsie! She had not even stirred.

'Good,' thought Carlotta, cuddling into bed. 'Everything went off marvelously. Oh, I wish we could have it all over again tomorrow night!'

The second-formers were very sleepy the next morning. They found it difficult to get up. Alison said she felt sick, and so did Katheleen.

'Well, never mind, it was worth it, wasn't it?' said Pat. 'Do you want to go to Matron?'

'No,' said Alison and Katheleen together. Matron would only give them a large dose of nasty-tasting medicine. She had an unfailing way of knowing when a midnight feast had been held, and kept special medicine for girls who complained of feeling sick the next day!

Elsie did not for one moment suspect that the feast had been held. Nobody said a word about it in front of her. The common room had been so well-cleared up that there was not a crumb left to give the secret away.

Elsie looked at the second-formers as they worked in Miss Jenks's geography class. 'You may think you are going to have a lovely time tonight!' she thought, 'but you won't! Miss Jenks will come and spoil it all—and that will serve you right for being so mean to me!'

Neither Alison nor Katheleen were sick after all, but because they would eat no breakfast and no dinner, Miss Jenks sent them to Matron. Matron took their temperatures, and found they had none.

'Hmmmm!' she said, thoughtfully. 'Any one had a birthday in the second form?'

'It's Carlotta's today,' said Katheleen.

'I thought so,' said Matron. 'You are both suffering from Too-Much-To-Eat. A dose of medicine will soon put you right!'

That night the second form went to bed with giggles and nudges. They felt quite certain Elsie was going to give them away—or was hoping to. They had made a lovely plan.

'We'll all wake up at midnight and creep out of the room,' planned Bobby. 'Then, as soon as we're gone, I bet Elsie will go off to tell Miss Jenks, or even Miss Theobald! You never know! When we see her go, we'll all creep back into bed and be there, pretending to be sound asleep, when Miss Jenks comes. What a sell for dear Elsie!'

Every one approved of this plan. Elsie saw them whispering and giggling, and felt certain it was about the feast that night! She made up her mind to keep awake, whatever happened.

Carlotta set her alarm clock for midnight once more–this time under her own pillow, as she wanted to make sure of waking Elsie up that night! It went off at twelve 'o'clock, and Carlotta sat up. She grinned to herself in the darkness.

She went from bed to bed, waking every one up, making rather a noise. Elsie woke up too, for she had fallen asleep after all. She pretended to lie fast asleep, and did not stir until all the girls had crept out of the dormitory. Then she sat up and pulled on her own dressing-gown.

'The beasts! Enjoying themselves without me!' she thought maliciously, forgetting that she could have joined in the party if she had said she would behave sensibly. 'Well, now I'll go and wake Miss Jenks—and pretend I'm frightened because the others have all disappeared!'

She slipped out of the dormitory. Carlotta who was hiding round a corner, saw her going down the passage in the opposite direction, on her way to Miss Jenks's room.

'Come along,' she whispered to the second-formers, who were giggling nearby. 'She's gone! I bet Miss Jenks will be along in half a minute! What will she say to Elsie when she sees us all safe and sound in our warm beds!'

The girls took off their dressing-gowns and slippers, and hurried back into their beds, which were still nice and warm. They cuddled down and waited, giggling every now and again when someone made a silly remark.

Meanwhile Elsie was knocking on Miss Jenks's door. There was no answer. She knocked more loudly. There was a creak from the bed and then Miss Jenks's voice. 'Who's there? What's the matter?'

Elsie opened the door. Miss Jenks switched on the light beside her bed. She saw Elsie, who had put on a very frightened expression indeed.

'Is somebody ill?' asked Miss Jenks, springing out of bed and dragging her dressing-gown on. 'Quick, tell me!'

'Oh, Miss Jenks—I'm so frightened,' stammered Elsie, filling Miss Jenks with foreboding, she looked so scared. 'All the girls out of my dormitory have disappeared—every one of them. Oh Miss Jenks—do you think they can have been kidnapped? I feel so scared.'

Miss Jenks snorted. She had a wonderful snort which was often faithfully copied by Doris.

'My dear Elsie, don't be a ninny! As if seven or eight girls could be kidnapped in your room and you hear nothing! Use your common sense, for pity's sake!'

'Miss Jenks, they really aren't there,' said Elsie, looking more wide-eyed than ever. 'Not one of them. Where can they be?'

'It's Carlotta's birthday, isn't it?' said Miss Jenks, crossly. 'I suppose it's a feast. Just like you to try and spoil it!'

'Oh, Miss Jenks, I never thought of that!' cried Elsie, pretending to be astonished and hurt. 'Oh, so long as they aren't kidnapped!'

'You really make me cross, Elsie,' said Miss Jenks, who, having had Elsie for more than a year in her form, knew her very well indeed. 'Well, come along—I suppose I'll have to look into this—but you'll just come along with me too, my girl—and the second form can see who's spoilt things for them!'

This was not what Elsie had planned at all! But it was no use, she could not draw back now. She had to go with Miss Jenks.

They went along to the dormitory where Elsie slept. The girls heard them coming and cuddled closer into bed, shutting their eyes tightly, hoping they would not giggle and give everything away. Doris gave one or two beautiful little snores, so real that Carlotta wondered if she could possibly have gone to sleep! Miss Jenks heard the snores. She switched on the dormitory light.

She stared in silence at the beds, all except Elsie's occupied by apparently sleeping girls. Doris gave another marvellous little snore, and then, with a realistic grunt, turned over in bed and settled down again. Miss Jenks watched her. She felt certain Doris was awake.

Elsie stared in the utmost astonishment and horror at the occupied beds. She simply could not understand it. She had not been more than three minutes away, surely—and yet here were all the girls asleep in bed. Could she have dreamt it all? Had the girls not stirred from their beds at all? What had happened?

'Well, Elsie,' said Miss Jenks, not troubling to lower her voice, for she felt certain every girl was awake, 'You appear to have brought me out on a wild-goose chase. We shall have to have a talk about this tomorrow, I think. I don't feel at all pleased to be woken up with a story of wholesale kidnappings, and then to find that the only girl out of bed is yourself. Not a very creditable performance on your part, I feel.'

Elsie got into bed without a word. Miss Jenks snapped off the light and went back to bed, shutting her ears to the giggling and whispering that immediately broke out. No one said a word to the cowering Elsie. Let her try to puzzle out what had happened! After ten minutes giggling the room went to sleep again—all but Elsie, who lay awake worrying about what was to happen to her the next day!

The first thing that happened had its funny side. Carlotta solemnly approached her and offered her a piece of the birthday cake. 'You weren't there, so we saved it for you,' she said, a very goody-goody expression on her glowing little face.

Elsie was startled out of her silence. She stared at the cake and said,' So you *did* have the feast after all? When did you?'

'We had it when we were kidnapped,' said Carlotta, solemnly. 'Oooh Elsie—it was thrilling! Somebody came in the middle of the night—and kidnapped us all—and took us away—but we offered them a bit of the birthday cake and they were so pleased with it that they set us free!'

'Don't tell such untruths!' said Elsie, angrily. There were squeals of laughter at this.

'Untruths! Why, who was it went and told Miss Jenks we had been kidnapped? *You* can't talk about untruths!'

Elsie turned away. She would not take the cake. She was sick at heart, and longed for a friendly look or a friendly word. Now she had to go and face Miss Jenks. That would be awful too. She had to go just before morning school, at ten minutes to nine in the classroom.

She went. Miss Jenks was there, busy as usual correcting piles of exercise books. On the desk in front of her was a most surprising sight—a large piece of birth-day cake! It had been offered to her by Carlotta with a merry twinkle––and had been accepted with a merry twinkle also! Elsie stared at it and bit her lip. To think that Miss Jenks had accepted the cake! Why, she must have guessed the feast-and here she was accepting a bit of the cake! It was too bad.

'Elsie, there is something seriously wrong with you this term,' began Miss Jenks. 'You had a great chance as head-girl, and both Miss Theobald and I hoped you would take it. Apparently you haven't. None of the girls will accept you. Instead of standing up to things and realizing you had to do better and change your attitude, you chose to do stupid things like coming to me last night with a cock-and-bull tale, in order to spite the others. They were too smart for you, I am pleased to see. Now what is to be done? Are you going to go on like this for the rest of the term? Your report will not make pleasant reading if so. Or are you going to show that you really have a little courage and common sense in you, and try to make up for your silly behaviour before it is too late?'

Plain speaking was Miss Jenks's strong point. Elsie listened in silence. She looked at the calm eyes of her form-mistress. There was absolutely nothing else to be done now but admit herself to be in the wrong, and say she had courage to do better. That was hard—but the alternative was harder—getting a thoroughly bad report, and having to bear the sneers of the girls for the rest of the term.

'I'll try to make up for being silly,' said Elsie, in a half-sulky tone.

'You've been more than silly,' said Miss Jenks. 'Pull yourself together. You know that St. Clare's only keeps the girls it can do something with. The second-formers are decent. If they see you showing a little courage and common sense, they will help you.'

'All right,' said Elsie, ungraciously. 'But, Miss Jenks—don't make me tell them I'm sorry or anything. I can't do that. I really can't.

'My dear Elsie, I haven't had you in my form for over a year without knowing that I can't expect you to have either the good feeling or the courage to say you're sorry,' said Miss Jenks, impatiently. 'Now here come the others. Go and get my books for me out of the mis-tresses' common room, and put on a little brighter face. I simply cannot bear to see you looking like a hen left out in the rain any longer!'

Elsie went to fetch Miss Jenks's books as the second-formers crowded into the room. They sat down at once, surprised to see their form-mistress there before them.

'I want to say a word to you this morning,' said Miss Jenks. 'About Elsie. She has agreed to try and have a little courage and go better from now on—rather unwillingly, I must admit. She tells me she cannot possibly say she is sorry to you for her stupid conduct—and in any case, I don't think she is sorry—but try to act towards her in a way to help her efforts, not hinder them, will you? After all —you played a wonderful trick on her last night, didn't you?'

This unexpected ending made all the girls smile delight-edly. So Miss Jenks guessed everything—and there was the birthday cake, sitting waiting to be eaten! Good old Miss Jenks! The girls were ready to do any-thing she asked them.

'All right, Miss Jenks—we'll put up with Elsie as graciously as we can,' said Hilary, smiling. 'We got our own back last night—so we can afford to be generous!'

Elsie came back into the room. She had tried to make her face pleasanter. She placed the books on the desk. 'Thank you, Elsie,' said Miss Jenks, in a pleasant tone, and gave her a smile. The girls saw it and approved. What Miss Jenks could do, they could do also. Things would be easier for Elsie than she deserved!

18   AN EXCITING MATCH

THE term went on its way, happy and busy with lessons, games and fun. Lacrosse matches were played, and the whole school turned out to watch and cheer at the home matches.

The second form were very proud of Gladys. Anna had told Miss Wilton, the games-mistress, that she thought Gladys would be worth trying in some other position than goal-keeper, and Miss Wilton rather doubtfully agreed to try her.

'She has never shown any aptitude for running, catching or tackling,' she said. 'However—we will see.'

So Gladys, to her delight, was put in position where running and catching would count, and after once or twice the girl proved herself to be very good. She was small, but very wiry and agile, and she was amazingly good at dodging the enemy and passing the ball quickly to some one else.

'Good, Gladys, good!' Miss Wilton said, time after time, one Monday afternoon. 'You *are* coming on!'

Gladys flushed with pleasure. She looked very happy these days. Miss Quentin was taking a good deal of notice of her in the Drama class, and now Miss Wilton was praising her at lacrosse—the two things she liked most. She was writing very happy letters to her mother now, and although she still had no reply, she had had a letter from Mirabel's mother that had delighted her.

DEAR GLADYS [the letter had said],

I thought you might like to know that I was able to go today to the hospital your mother is in. The nurse actually allowed me to see her for two minutes, as it was one of her good days. I told her about you, and how you and my Mirabel were friends. She could not say much, but she did say how delighted she was to hear what a success you were at the concert. Perhaps you will be able to see her in the holidays. It is early days to say yet whether she is really making progress, but I think you may be hopeful. I will go see her again if I can.

Give my love to Mirabel, and say I hope she is treating you properly! You are such a little mouse and Mirabel is just the opposite!

Love from,
ELISE UNWIN

This letter Gladys treasured greatly. She thought with intense gratitude of Mrs. Unwin. She began to hope that her mother really might get better. She knew that when she was well enough she had to have a serious operation, and this thought worried her greatly—but now that she was happier things did not seem so bad.

Meantime there was lacrosse, and the excitement of the next match, which was to be a home one, against St. Christopher's. Belinda Towers had let it be known that she would like to choose one girl from the second form for the team. No one in the first form was good enough as yet-but the second form were on the whole not at all bad at the game.

'*You* might be chosen, Gladys!' said Mirabel, half teasingly. She did not seriously think that the shy girl would be picked out, for although she certainly was very good at the game now, she was not half the size of some of the other girls in the form.

'I wish I could!' said Gladys. 'But I know who will be—Hilary! She's terribly good, I think.'

Hilary certainly was very good—very sure and very swift. Her catching was graceful to watch, and it seemed certain she would be chosen for the match.

But two days before the match Hilary went down with a cold again. Matron popped her into bed, in spite of her wails about lacrosse.

'Belinda said I could play in the match!' she said. 'Can't I get up tomorrow for certain?'

'Nothing is certain with bad colds,' said Matron. 'So don't count on anything.'

Thus it came about that Hilary, although chosen by Belinda, could not play—and Belinda, running her pencil down the list of names in the second form, suddenly came to a stop by Gladys Hillman's name. She sat and thought.

'That kids's good,' thought the head-girl. 'I watched her yesterday. She's fast—and jolly good at tackling, although she is small. I've a good mind to try her.'

So, when the list of names was put up on the big notice-board, showing the girls chosen for the next match, Gladys Hillman's appeared at the bottom—the only one chosen from the second from! Mirabel saw it and went hurriedly in search of Gladys.

'Gladys! What do you think? You're down for the match!'

'Really?' said Gladys, her face flushing brightly. 'Oh—how marvellous! Golly, I *shall* be nervous, though!'

'No, you won't. You'll just remember that your mother is longing to hear that you've shot twelve goals for St. Clare's, and that you've won the match for the school!' said Mirabel, laughing. 'Oh, I say—I am pleased. Good for you!'

Gladys was happy to see Mirabel's real pleasure. That was the best of friends—they shared your troubles with you, and they doubled your joys. It was good to have a friend.

The school turned out as usual to watch the match. The St. Christopher girls came in a big coach, their lacrosse sticks beside them. The St. Clare's girls gave them a cheer.

The game began. Belinda was referee, and blew her whistle sharply. There was the click of lacrosse sticks as the two girls in the centre of the field began the game. Then the ball was flicked quickly away, and Margery Fenworthy, of the third form, picked it up in her lacrosse net and flew down the field with it. She passed to Lucy Oriell, her friend, and then when Lucy was tackled, cleverly caught the ball once more and passed to Gladys, who was hopping about in excitement, ready for any chance.

Click! Gladys caught the ball, dodged a tackling enemy, and threw to Lucy. From one to another went the

ball, and Lucy tried to throw a goal, which was deftly
stopped by the St. Christopher's goal-keeper.

The game was very even. The St. Clare girls were
better runners and catchers, but the St. Christopher goal-
keeper was marvellous. She had a quick eye, a firm
wrist, and a real talent for stopping the ball every time
the St. Clare girls threw at the goal.

St. Christopher's threw a goal first, and the St. Clare
girls clapped, though their faces were rather anxious.
This was going to be a stiffer match than they thought.
Thank goodness both Margery Fenworthy and Lucy
Oriell were playing today—they were always first-class.
Some of the St. Clare girls looked doubtfully at Gladys
Hillman. She seemed very small in comparison with the
others. Margery Fenworthy, for instance, was a big strap-
ping girl who over-topped Gladys by a head and a half!

'Play up, Gladys!' yelled Mirabel, every time her friend
came near her. 'Go on—play up!'

And the whole second form would yell in chorus.
'Play up, Gladys! What about a goal from you?'

Half-time—and no goals for the St. Clare girls! One-
love! The St. Clare girls who were watching crowded
round their team, trying to buck them up and spur them on.

'You are doing well, Margery and Lucy,' said
Belinda Towers, approvingly. Her eye caught the flushed
face of Gladys Hillman, and she gave her one of her sudden
wide smiles. 'You're not doing too badly either, kid! But
keep a bit a closer to Margery, will you? You might be able
to score a goal off one of her passes to you.'

'Yes, Belinda,' said Gladys, happily. 'I'll try.' She kept
her word. She hovered closer to Margery, and caught the
ball slickly each time. Twice she was tackled and had to
pass before she could shoot at the goal—but the third she
threw the ball with all her might at the net in the distance.

'Goal, goal' yelled the St. Clare girls. But no, the St.

Christopher goal-keeper deftly flicked the ball away. No goal—but a jolly good try!

'Go it, Gladys, go it!' yelled the second form, dancing about in excitement. 'Try again!'

Gladys did her best. She was everywhere, in and out, running, tackling, passing. Time slipped on, and still no goals were scored by St. Clare's. On the other hand no more were scored by St. Christopher's, either. It was the closet match the schools had ever played.

'Oh golly, it's almost time!' groaned Mirabel, glancing at her watch. 'Gladys! Play up. There's only four minutes more!'

Gladys heard, and ran to tackle an enormous St. Christopher girl. The girl dodged, and Gladys tripped. She wrenched her ankle, and gave a groan. It was going to be painful to run now. But she couldn't possibly give up!

The ball rolled near her. She nipped it up into her lacrosse net, and ran, limping, down the field. She passed to Margery, who at once passed back again when she was tackled. Gladys didn't catch the ball. It was neatly caught by a much taller girl, who leapt into the air. The ball fell into her net, and she turned to run down the field. But quick as thought Gladys hit her lacrosse stick upwards, and the ball flew into the air. Gladys caught it, and ran again. She shot for the goal.

It was not such a good shot as before—but the ball bounced over a tuff as it rolled towards the goal, and avoided the waiting lacrosse net of the goal-keeper. In the greatest dismay she saw it roll into the goal!

The St. Clare girls nearly went mad with joy. The second form thumped each other on the back and yelled "Good old Gladys" at the tops of their voices. It was all very thrilling.

The match was a draw-one all. The St. Christopher

Gladys raced after the ball

girls went back to tea with St. Clare's, and discussed the
match at the tops of their voices. The second form treated
Gladys to a special cake for making the score even.

'Good for you, kid!' said Belinda, as she passed. That
was Gladys' biggest reward! Words of praise from the
great head-girl were words of praise indeed!

19   ALISON AND MISS QUENTIN

THE term hurried on its way. The girls began to talk about
Christmas holidays and what they were going to do—
pantomimes, parties and theatres were discussed. Gladys
looked a little bleak when the girls began to talk excitedly
about coming holidays.

'Will your mother be well enough to leave the hospital and have you home with her?' asked Mirabel.

'No. I'm staying at school for hols.,' said Gladys.
'Matron will still be here, you know, and two girls from the
third and fourth form, whose parents are in India. But I
shall be very lonely without you, Mirabel.'

'Poor Gladys!' said Mirabel in dismay. 'I should
hate to stay at school for the hols. I must say. After all,
most of the fun of being at boarding-school is being
with crowds of others, day and night—it won't be any fun
for you being with one or two! Won't your mother really
be better?'

'She's going to have a serious operation soon,' said

Gladys. 'So I know quite well she won't be able to leave the hospital, Mirabel. But the operation may make her well again, so I'm just hoping for the best—and I'm quite willing to stay on at school for the hols. If only I hear that Mother is getting better after the operation.'

Mrs. Unwin had written to Mirabel about Gladys's mother. She had told Mirabel not to show the letter to Gladys.

'I feel rather worried about Gladys's mother,' she wrote. 'She is to have the operation soon-and I can't help wondering if she really will get over it, because she is very weak. If there is bad news, you must comfort Gladys all you can. She will be very glad to have a friend if sadness comes to her. I will let her know at once if the news is good.'

Mirabel said nothing to her friend about the letter—but she was extra warm and friendly towards Gladys. It was unusual for the rather selfish, thick-skinned Mirabel to think of some one else unselfishly and tenderly. It softened her domineering nature and made her a much nice girl.

Gladys was pleased to be able to tell her mother about the match. She wished she had shot a winning goal-but it was something to shoot the goal that made a draw!

'*I* shall write and tell your mother too,' said Mirabel, who could not do enough for her friend just then.

'Oh Mirabel—you are good!' said Gladys, delighted. 'You wrote to Mother after the concert, and I guess she was pleased to hear all you said. My word—what a silly I was at the beginning of the term, all mopey and miserable, couldn't take an interest in anything. I should think you hated me.'

'Well. I didn't like you very much,' said Mirabel, honestly. 'But I guess you didn't like *me* much, either!'

Gladys was not only shining at lacrosse but in the Drama

class as well! Miss Quentin, who had been really amazed at Gladys's performance on the night of the concert, was making a great fuss of her and her talent. Alison didn't like it at all. She was jealous, and there were some days when she could hardly speak to Gladys.

The play was to be performed at the end of the term. Miss Quentin had tried out Alison, Doris, Carlotta, and now Gladys in the principal feminine part. There was no doubt that Alison looked the prettiest and the most graceful, and that she was quite word-perfect and had rehearsed continually. But Gladys was by far the best actress.

Miss Quentin had given Alison to understand that she would have the chief part. She had not actually said so in so many words, but the class as a whole took it for granted that Alison would take the part. They found it quite natural too, for they knew how hard the girl had worked at learning the words, a task always difficult for her.

Alison was really silly about Miss Quentin. She waited round corners for her, hoping for a smile. She hung on every word the teacher said. She was worse than she had been with Sadie Greene the term before-for one thing Sadie had had a little common sense and often laughed at Alison, but Miss Quentin had no common sense at all! So Alison became worse instead of better, and the second-formers became quite exasperated with her.

Then Alison heard some news that gave her a great blow—Miss Quentin was not coming back the next term!

'Are you sure?' asked Alison, looking with wide eyes at Hilary, who had come in with the news.

'Well, I heard Mam'zelle say to Miss Quentin, 'Well, well—so you will be on the stage next term, whilst we are all struggling with our tiresome girls!' Apparently Miss Quentin had only just heard the news herself—she had a

letter in her hand. I think she must only have been engaged
for a term—it's the first time we've had a proper Drama
class. Perhaps Miss Theobald was trying out the idea.'
Hilary looked at Alison, who had tears in her eyes. 'Cheer
up, Alison—the world won't come to an end because your
beloved Miss Quentin isn't here next term! You'll find some
one else to moon round, don't fret!'

It was a great shock to Alison. She had dreamed of
term after term in Miss Quentin's Drama classes, with herself taking all the chief parts in every play, hearing honeyed
words of praise daily from the teacher's lips. She went
away by herself and cried very bitterly. The silly girl gave
her heart far too easily to anyone who attracted her, or
made a fuss of her.

'What's come over Alison?' asked Pat, in surprise,
when her cousin appeared with swollen eyes. 'Been in
a row, Alison?'

'She's only sorrowing because her beloved Miss
Quentin won't be here next term to pat her back and tell
her she is very very good!' said Janet.

'Alison, don't be an idiot!' said Isabel. 'You know perfectly well Miss Quentin won't be much loss. We all think
she's too soft for words! And think how mean she was in
taking the credit for Gladys's performance at the concert.'

'I have never believed that,' said Alison, tears coming
into her eyes again. 'You don't know Miss Quentin as I
do—she's the truest, honestest, most loyal person! I've
never met any one like her.'

'Nor have I!' said Pat. 'And thank goodness I haven't.
Alison, why must you do and choose the wrong people to
moon round? Sadie Greene was amusing but she hadn't
anything in her at all—and neither has Miss Quentin. Now,
take Miss Jenks for instance...'

'Miss Jenks!' said Alison, with an angry sniff. 'Who
would want to moon round Miss Jenks, with her snappy

tongue and cold eyes?'

'Well, I think she's pretty decent,' said Pat. 'Not that I should want to moon round her or any one, for that matter. I'm only just saying you will keep on choosing the wrong people to lavish your affections on! Sadie has never even written to you—and I bet Miss Quentin won't, either!'

'She will! She's very fond of me,' said Alison.

The others gave it up. Alison would never learn sense! 'It's pity she can't find out how silly her Miss Quentin really is—how undependable,' said Hilary. 'Your feather-headed cousin, Pat, wants to learn common sense —it's pity she can't find out that all her ideas about Miss Quentin are only dreams—the real Miss Quentin isn't a bit as Alison pictures her!'

'Well, we can't teach her,' said Pat. 'She'll make herself miserable for the rest of the term now, and for all the hols. too, I expect!'

Alison was really unhappy to hear that her favourite teacher was leaving. She thought she would hang about near the common room of the Junior mistresses, and watch for Miss Quentin to come out. Then she would tell her how upset she was.

So she went to a little lobby near the common room, and pretended to be hunting for something there. She could hear Miss Quentin's voice talking to Mam'zelle, behind the closed door of the common room, but she could not hear anything that was said.

Then some one opened the door and came out. It was Miss Lewis, the history teacher. 'Leave the door open!' cried Mam'zelle, 'it is stuffy in here!'

So Miss Lewis left the door open, and went off towards the school library. Alison stood in the little lobby, her heart beating fast, waiting for Miss Quentin to come out. Surely she would come soon!

The mistresses went on talking. Some of them had clear, distinct voices, and some spoke too low for Alison to hear anything. She did not mean to listen, she was only waiting for Miss Quentin—but suddenly she heard her own name, spoken by Miss Quentin herself. Alison stiffened, and her heart thumped. Was Miss Quentin going to praise her to the others? It would be just like her to stay something nice!

'Alison O'Sullivan is going to get a shock,' said Miss Quentin, in the low, clear voice that Alison thought so beautiful. 'The silly girl thinks she's good enough to play the lead in the second-form play! She's been wearing herself out rehearsing—it will do her good to find she's not going to have the part!'

'Who's going to have it, then?' asked Miss Jenks.

'Gladys Hillman,' answered Miss Quentin, promptly. 'I've had my eye on that child ever since the beginning of the term. She's three times as good as any one else. She will be marvellous as the Countess Jeannette.'

'I wish Alison worked as hard in my classes as she does in yours,' remarked Mam'zelle, in her rather harsh, loud voice. 'Ah, her French exercise! But I think, Miss Quentin, she really does work at Drama.'

'Oh well, she simply adores me,' said Miss Quentin, easily. 'I can always make her type work. She'll do anything for a smile or a kind word from me—like a dear little pet-dog. But give me somebody like that wild Carlotta— somebody with something in them! Alison bores me to tears with her breathless 'Yes, Miss Quentin! No, Miss Quentin!' 'Oh, *can* I, Miss Quentin!' It will be good for her to have a shock and find she has to take back place to Gladys Hillman.'

'I'm not so sure,' said Miss Jenks, in her cool voice. 'Shocks are not always good for rather weak characters, Miss Quentin. I hope you will break your news kindly to poor Alison—otherwise she will weep all day, and as exams. are coming on tomorrow, I don't want bad work from her because of you!'

'Oh don't worry! I'll just pat her curly head and say a few kind words,' said Miss Quentin. 'She'll eat out of my hand. She always does.'

Miss Lewis came back and shut the door. Not a word more could be heard. Alison sat on a bench in the lobby sick at heart, shocked and hurt beyond measure. Her mind was in a whirl. She had not been able to help hearing—and once she had grasped that her idol, Miss Quentin, was poking fun at her, she had not even been able to get up and go. She had had to sit there, hearing every cruel word.

She was not to have the leading part in the play. Miss Quentin wasn't fond of her—only amused with her, thinking her a little pet-dog, some one to pat and laugh at! Miss Quentin had told a lie—she had not noticed Gladys Hillman at all until the night of the concert! Miss Quentin was bored with her!

Alison was too shocked even to cry. She sat in the lobby quietly, looking straight in front of her. What was it that Miss Jenks had said? 'Shocks are not always good for weak characters!' Was she, Alison, such a weak character then? The girl rubbed her hand across her forehead, which was wet and clammy.

'I have to think all this out,' said Alison to herself. 'I can't tell any one. I'm too ashamed. But I must think things out. Oh, Miss Quentin, how could you say all that?'

Poor Alison! This was the greatest shock she had ever had in her easy-going life! All her admiration and love for Miss Quentin vanished at once—passed like a dream in the night. There was nothing of it left, except an ache. She saw the Drama teacher as the others saw her—some one pleasant and amiable, but undependable, disloyal, shallow.

Alison was a silly girl, as changeable as a weather-vane, swinging now this way and now that, easily upset and easily pleased. As the others often said, 'she hadn't much in her!' But in this hour of horror—for it was horror to her—she found something in herself that she hardly knew she possessed. And that something was a sense of dignity!

She wasn't going to go under because of some one like Miss Quentin! She wasn't going to be a pet-dog, eating out of her hand! She had too much dignity for that. She would show Miss Quentin that she was wrong. Hurt and shocked though she was, Alison had a glimmering of common sense all at once, and she held up her head, blinked away the tears, and made up her mind what she was going to do.

So it came about that when Miss Quentin broke the news to the Drama class that Gladys was to have the leading part, and not Alison, the girl gave no sign at all of being disappointed. Her face was pale, for she had slept badly that night, but it had a calmness and dignity that astonished the watching girls.

'So Gladys is to have the part, you see,' finished Miss Quentin. She lightly touched Alison's curly head. 'I'm afraid my Alison will be disappointed!'

'Of course not, Miss Quentin,' said Alison, moving away from the teacher's hand. 'I think Gladys *should* have the part! She is the best of us all—and I am very glad.'

The girls stared at Alison in the greatest amazement. They had expected tears—even sulks—but not this cool acceptance of an unpleasant fact.

'Who would have thought Alison would take it like that?' said Janet. 'Well—good for her! All the same, I think it's a shame. Miss Quentin made us all think Alison would have the part.'

Alison would not meet Miss Quentin eye. She played the part she was given very well, but seemed quite unmoved when Miss Quentin praised her. Miss Quentin was puzzled and a little hurt.

'Girls, I have something to tell you,' she said at the end of the lesson. 'I shall not be here next term. I shall miss you all very much—especially one or two of you who have worked extremely hard!'

She looked hard at Alison, expecting to see tears, and to hear cries of 'Oh, Miss Quentin! We shall miss you!'

But Alison did not look at the teacher. She gazed out of the window as if she had not heard. Hilary cleared her throat and spoke politely. 'I am sure we are all sorry to hear that, Miss Quentin. We hope you will be happy wherever you go.'

Miss Quentin was hurt and disappointed. She spoke directly to Alison.

'Alison, I know you worked specially hard for me,' she said.

'I worked hard because I like Drama,' said Alison, in a cool voice, looking Miss Quentin in the eyes for the first time. This was a direct snub and the girls gasped in surprise. Whatever made Alison behave like that? They gazed at her in admiration. So Alison had seen through her beloved Miss Quentin at last—and instead of moaning and wailing, had put on a cloak of dignity and coolness. One up to Alison!

Miss Quentin retired gracefully to her next class, very much puzzled. The girls crowded round Alison.

'Alison! What's happened? Has your beloved Miss Quentin offended you?'

'Shut up,' said Alison, pushing her way between the girls. 'I can't tell you anything. I don't want to discuss it. Let me alone.'

They let her go, puzzled, but respecting her request. 'Something's happened,' said Hilary, watching the white-faced girl going out of the room. 'But whatever it is, is for the best. Alison seems suddenly more grown-up.'

'Time she was,' said Pat. 'Anyway—if she stops mooning round somebody different each term—or at any rate chooses somebody worth-while—it will be a blessing!'

Nobody ever knew what had made Alison 'grow up' so suddenly. Only Alison herself knew, and out of her hurt came something worth-while, that was to help her in many years to come.

EXAMS. were being held, and girls were groaning daily over them. Mam'zelle was in a state of trepidation in case any of the girls fell short of pass-marks. The girls were in a far greater state, feeling quite certain that nobody at all would pass in French! Mam'zelle always threatened to give them such difficult papers-but when the time came, they were not so bad after all!

Gladys found the exams. difficult because her mother was to have her operation that week. She was very anxious indeed. Mirabel did all she could to help her to prepare each evening. It was good to see the patience and kindliness of the bigger girl. The others warmed greatly to Mirabel because of it.

Even Elsie felt sorry for the anxious girl. 'I hope you'll hear good news soon,' she said. Gladys looked at her in surprised gratitude. Fancy Elsie saying anything kind! The others heard the low words, and looked at one another with raised eyebrows. They had kept their promise to Miss Jenks, and had not hindered Elsie in any way, in her efforts to behave more reasonably.

But, on the other hand, no girl had been able to show any liking for Elsie. It was impossible. The girl had been too spiteful, too exasperating altogether to be liked now. She would be tolerated, but nothing else. Miss Jenks watched every one's behaviour, and came to the conclusion that it was hopeless to expect any happiness or real help for Elsie from the second-formers. On the other hand, the lazy Anna had been a great success as head-girl of the form. She had thrown aside her laziness, and had to the fore, taking responsibility and making decisions capably and quickly. Miss Jenks was pleased with her. She was now ready to go up into the third form, and take her part with the older girls there. Hilary Wentworth could be head-girl next term.

Miss Jenks spoke to Miss Theobald about it and the Head agreed. 'But what are we to do with Elsie?' she said. 'I will have a talk with her.'

So Elsie was sent for, and sat rather sullenly in Miss Theobald's drawing-room, expecting to be scolded, or something even worse—she might be told that St. Clare's didn't want her any more!

'Elsie,' said Miss Theobald, 'I know you have found things difficult this term—mostly your own fault, as I think you will admit.'

Elsie looked at Miss Theobald's solemn face. 'Yes,' she said at last. 'I suppose things were mostly my own fault. The second form don't like me at all. They will never have me as head-girl. They just tolerate me, that's all. It makes things hard for me. I feel I can never do anything to alter their opinion, and so I can't very well take any pleasure in being there.'

'You see, Elsie, one of the hardest things in the world to forget and forgive is spitefulness,' said Miss Theobald. 'Malice and spite rouse such bitter feelings in others. Other faults, such as greed, irresponsibility, silli-ness—these arouse disgust, but are forgotten and forgiven. Spite always rankles, and is never forgotten. I can see you will never do any good either to yourself or to others in the second form.'

Elsie waited, her heart sinking. This meant that she was to be asked to leave. She didn't want to do that. She did like St. Clare's. She stared at Miss Theobald miserably. The Head guessed what the girls was think-ing.

'I'm not going to say you must leave St. Clare's,' she

said quickly. 'I think the school can do a lot for you, Elsie, and you may be able to do something for St. Clare's too. No-you shan't leave! Think you must go up into the third form instead—leave behind the second—formers who have seen such a bad side of your character-and go into the third form, which, next term, will have five or six new girls. You will have a chance then to show a different side of your character! You are not really ready to go up, either in your work, or in your behaviour—but I will send you up if you will tell me that you will take this chance, and work hard, and more important still, try to get the "cattiness" out of your nature that every schoolgirl detests!'

Elsie's heart lifted in relief. Go up into the third form—and leave behind the girls who would always dislike her! Would she work hard! Wouldn't she be kind and friendly and helpful to the new girls who didn't know anything about her! She smiled gladly.

'What about Anna?' she asked. 'Is she going up too?'

"Yes—but you can trust Anna not to give you away at all,' said Miss Theobald. 'She's a good girl—she really has turned out well as head-girl. Now, Elsie—take this chance and make good!'

'I will,' said Elsie. 'Thank you, Miss Theobald. I never thought of going up into the third form! It makes all the difference in the world!'

The girl went out, pleased and hopeful. She saw Gladys Hillman in the passage and went up to her with a warm gesture of friendliness.

'Any news of your mother, old thing?' she asked.

'Not yet,' said Gladys, wondering whatever could have made Elsie look so friendly and glad. Elsie went on her way and met Bobby.

'I say,' she said, 'I saw poor old Gladys just now. Can't we do something to take her out of herself a bit? She's moping again.'

'Good idea!' said Bobby at once. 'I'll play that trick on Mam'zelle—you know, the trick that makes plates jump about! Mam'zelle is taking lunch today at our table, because Miss Jenks is going out. It will be sport!'

So the second-formers were told that a trick was about to be played, and they all cheered up, forgot about exams., and looked at Bobby with bright eyes. The first trick that term! It was time one was played!

Mam'zelle was in a good temper. The first form had done unexpectedly well in their French exam. She beamed at everybody. The second-formers beamed back and Doris gave a deep chuckle, exactly like Mam'zelle's.

'Ah, this bad Doris!' said Mam'zelle, clapping Doris on the shoulder. 'She can imitate me perr-r-rfectly—but she cannot roll her's yet in the true French way! Now—let us go to the dining-room. The bell for luncheon has gone. Today I take you for the meal, because the good Miss Jenks is out!'

The second form seated themselves at their table. Mam'zelle was at the head. Bobby was three places away from her. The others looked at her, grinning. They hoped she had been able to slip into the dining-room and lay her plans!

Bobby had prepared everything carefully. There was a pile of plates at Mam'zelle's place, ready for her to serve the stew for each girl. Bobby had removed the plates, and had deftly placed the long rubber tubing under the table-cloth, so that it ran from where the plates were to Bobby's own seat, and hung down under the cloth. The bladder-end was where the plates were, and the bulb to press was by Bobby's place. Bobby replaced the pile of plates over the bladder-end. The plates were too heavy to move when the bulb was pressed—but when all the girls, were served and only Mam'zelle plate was there, it would tip up beautifully as soon as Bobby pressed the bulb which filled the bladder-end with air!

Mam'zelle served out the stew rapidly. The girls began their meal hungrily, one eye on Mam'zelle's plate. It was the only one left now. Mam'zelle filled it with stew and gravy. She was very fond of gravy.

'At first,' said Mam'zelle conversationally, taking up her knife and fork, 'at first when I came to England I did not like this stew of yours! But now—ah, it is wonderful!'

Bobby pressed the rubber bulb she was holding under the cloth. The bladder-end under Mam'zelle's plate filled with air and became fat and big. Mam'zelle's plate tilted up on one side, gave a little wobble and subsided again as Bobby let go the bulb she was pressing.

Mam'zelle was overcome with astonishment. She left her nose to see if her glasses were there. Yes, they were. But could she have seen right? Her plate had moved!

She took a quick look round at the girls. They seemed to have noticed nothing—though actually all the girls had seen the plate lift and wobble, and were fighting hard to keep from giggling.

Mam'zelle dismissed the matter from her mind. She had imagined it! She began to make conversation again.

'Tomorrow you second-formers will have your French test,' she said, smiling round. Then she tried to cut a piece of meat with her knife-whilst Bobby at the same moment pressed the rubber bulb. Air ran through to the bladder, and Mam'zelle's plate lifted itself up very suddenly, and split some gravy over one side.

Mam'zelle looked at her plate in alarm. It had done it again. It was alive! It had split its gravy on the cloth.

'*Tiens*!' said Mam'zelle, very much startled. 'What is this!'

'What is what, Mam'zelle?' asked Janet, with a solemn face.

'Nothing, nothing!' said Mam'zelle, hastily, not liking to say that she feared her plate was alive. But something certainly was the matter with it. She looked down at it, hardly daring to eat her meal.

Bobby gave the plate a rest. Mam'zelle looked at it warily for a little while, and then plucked up her courage to eat her meal once more. The plate seemed to be behaving itself. Then it suddenly went mad again!

It tipped up and down slowly and solemnly three times, then jerked from side to side spilling some more gravy. Mam'zelle grew really alarmed. She glanced at the girls. How strange that they did not seem to see what was happening! She must be going mad!

'Don't you like your stew, Mam'zelle?' asked Pat, solemnly. 'I thought you said it was wonderful.'

Mam'zelle looked suspiciously at her plate which was now quiet. Doris made a silly joke in order to let the girls laugh loudly, for two or three of them were almost hysterical by now, and would certainly have given the game away if they had not been able to laugh loudly.

The rest of the school looked in amazement at the bellowing girls. Miss Theobald, who sat at the head of the sixth-form table, was displeased.

'Quiet, please,' she called to the second-formers. They choked and became quiet. Doris was purple in the face with trying not to laugh again. Mam'zelle looked round with a frown.

'Such a noise!' she said, reprovingly. But her attention was soon drawn to her plate again when it solemnly rose up and down twice, and then became quite still.

Mam'zelle frowned. This could not really be happening! Plates could not behave like that. It was nonsense. She would eat her dinner and not think about it.

'Don't do it again till the pudding comes,' whispered Carlotta to Bobby. 'We can't help squealing with laughter now. We shall get into a row. Give us—a rest!'

So for the rest of first course the plate behaved itself, and Mam'zelle was much relieved. But when the pudding arrived, and she had served it out, leaving only her own plate in its place, the fun began again. The pudding-plate leapt quite wildly, and Mam'zelle pushed her chair back with a scream. The girls choked and the tears ran down their cheeks.

'Ah! This plate!' cried Mam'zelle.' It is as bad as the other one. See how it jumps!'

Bobby kept the plate quite still. Doris exploded into laughter and two or three joined her helplessly. Miss Theobald began to look really vexed. The rest of the school craned their necks to see whatever could be happening at the second-form table.

The plate moved again, and Mam'zelle backed away still farther. Miss Theobald, amazed and puzzled, left her place and walked over to the second-form table. Every girl was rocking in helpless laughter. Not even the presence of the Head Mistress could stop them. This was the funniest thing they had ever seen.

'Mam'zelle! What is the matter?' asked Miss Theobald, really annoyed. Mam'zelle turned to her wildly.

'My plate!' she said. 'My plate!'

'Well, what is wrong with it?' asked Miss Theobald, impatiently, thinking that Mam'zelle must really have gone mad. 'It seems all right to me.'

'Miss Theobald, it jumps, it dances, it leaps around the table,' said Mam'zelle, earnestly, exaggerating in the hope that Miss Theobald would be impressed. 'It is a mad plate. I cannot bear it.'

The Head Mistress looked at the plate of pudding. It

lay quite still on the table, perfectly ordinary. She glanced round at the giggling girls. She supposed they were laughing at Mam'zelle's behaviour. Well, it certainly was extraordinary.

'You had better go and lie down, Mam'zelle,' she said at last. 'I think you can't be well.'

'*I* am well,' said poor Mam'zelle. 'It is the plate that is mad. You should see it jump, Miss Theobald.'

Miss Theobald looked doubtfully at the plate—and Bobby had a tremendous urge to make it jump again. She pressed the bulb hard, and the plate jumped up at once, wobbled and fell back again. Miss Theobald looked astonished and Mam'zelle gave another squeal. The girls screamed with laughter.

Miss Theobald lifted up the plate, and pushed back the table-cloth. There, underneath, was the little rubber bladder attached to the tubing that led to Bobby's place. Mam'zelle eyes nearly fell out of her head when she saw it.

'I think, Mam'zelle, one of the girls is playing a trick on you,' said Miss Theobald. 'I will leave you to deal with it. I daresay Roberta can explain how it was done.'

The girls stopped laughing. They stared at Miss Theobald walking back to her seat. They looked at Mam'zelle who glared at poor Bobby.

'What is this horrible trick?' she inquired in a loud voice.

Bobby explained, and Mam'zelle listened carefully. She removed the whole thing and looked at it. Then she put back the table-cloth and her plate and began to eat her pudding, looking straight in front of her with her sole-black eyes.

The girls felt uncomfortable. Was Mam'zelle really offended, really angry? The trick was quite a harmless one. They finished their pudding and sat still.

Suddenly there came a snort from Mam'zelle and all the

second-formers looked up in surprise. Mam'zelle threw back her head. She roared, she bellowed! She laughed so much that the relieved second-formers couldn't help laughing again too.

'It was a good trick,' said Mam'zelle at last, wiping her eyes. 'Yes, a good trick. I shall make my sister laugh till she cries when I tell her. When I think of that plate jumping at me like that—ah, *magnifique!*'

'I'll lend you the whole trick, if *you like*,' said Janet. 'It belongs to my brother. You can play the trick on your sister.'

Mam'zelle stared at her in delight. 'What a good idea!' she exclaimed, beaming. 'This will cheer my good sister immensely. You shall show me how it works.'

Miss Theobald smiled as she left the room. It really had been funny. What a good thing Mam'zelle had seen the funny side—but she could generally be trusted to. Poor Mam'zelle—the hundreds of tricks that had been played on her during her years at St. Clare's! She would never learn to be suspicious of the girls!

'Marvellous!' said Janet, when the second-formers were in their common room again, discussing the affair. 'Simply super. Bobby, you did it awfully well. I thought I should have died, trying to keep in my laughter. Oh, dear—when I think of that plate jumping about—and Mam'zelle's horrified face—I want to scream all over again!'

Every one was amused, and Gladys, who had seen few tricks played in her life, laughed as much as any one. She forgot her worry for a while, and Mirabel was glad to see her smiling as she listened to the talk.

The next day Mam'zelle gave out the French papers. They were much easier than the class expected and every one gave a sigh of relief. Even Doris hoped she might get enough marks for a pass!

In the middle of the exam. when everything was perfectly quiet, some one flashed by the window on a bicycle. Mirabel glanced up. It was a telegraph boy! She looked across at Gladys. Gladys had seen him too and had gone white. She wondered if the telegram held any news for her.

After a few minutes the door opened and a maid looked in. 'Please could Miss Gladys Hillman go to Miss Theobald,' she said. Gladys stood up, her knees shaking. She was sure the telegram said that her mother was dead. She went out of the room as if she was walking in a dream. Mirabel stared after her, miserable. She feared the worst too.

But in two minutes Gladys was back! The door was flung open, and she burst into the room, her face beaming, and her eyes shining. She rushed to Mirabel.

'Mirabel! Mother's had the operation, and she's come through it wonderfully! She's going to get better! I'm to see her soon, just for an hour! Perhaps next week, Mirabel! Isn't it marvellous!'

Mirabel was a glad as if it had been her own mother. She forgot about the class, and put her arm around the happy girl.

'Oh, Gladys!' she said. 'It's marvellous! I am glad!'

'Hurrah!' yelled Bobby, as delighted as any one. 'Good old Gladys!'

'I too am glad,' beamed Mam'zelle, forgetting all about the French exam., for a wonder. 'Such a surprise for you! Now you will be able to smile again!'

Gladys glanced round the room, suddenly remembering where she was. She had forgotten everything for the moment except that she must tell Mirabel, her friend, the great news. She went back to her seat, so happy that she felt she might cry with gladness at any moment.

'And now, we must look at our exam. papers again,'

said Mam'zelle, in a kindly voice. 'Gladys, you should do a wonderful paper, with such good news to help you!'

Every one was glad. The term had only two more days to go, and the girls were pleased to think that Gladys had something to look forward to. They were as nice to her as they could be, even Elsie!

The last day came, and packing began. Gladys couldn't help feeling a little sad as she saw every one preparing to go away for the holidays. She would have to stay at school —but, never mind, she would be able to see her mother soon. What a pity she was so far away- it would be difficult to see her more than once.

Just as the second form were in a complete muddle over their packing. Miss Theobald came into the room with a letter in her hand. She had just received it. The girls stood up and listened.

'Oh, Mirabel,' said Miss Theobald in her clear voice, 'I have just received a letter from your mother. She says you can take Gladys home with you for the holidays if I will give my permission, as then she can go to see her mother twice a week quite easily from your home, which is not very far from the hospital.'

Mirabel gave a shriek of delight. Gladys turned as red as a beetroot.

'Miss Theobald! How marvellous! Isn't mother a brick? Can Gladys come with me?'

'Of course,' said the Head Mistress, smiling at the bewildered, radiant Gladys. 'But she will have to pack very quickly. Hurry up, Gladys, and see if you can be ready by the time the school-coaches arrive!'

Ready! Of course she could be ready! Helped by willing hands Gladys flew here and there, cramming everything in, her heart singing with joy. To go home with Mirabel —see her friend's brother and sister—visit her own mother twice a week! What wonderful luck!

'And if I hadn't tackled Mirabel that time, and got her to change her mind and stay on, nothing like this would have happened!' thought the girl, packing her jerseys. 'It just shows you've got to have courage and go straight for things. Oh, it's too good to be true!'

But it was true, and Gladys went off in the school-coach with Mirabel beside her, singing heartily with the others as they rolled down to the station. Alison clapped her on the back. 'Happy holidays, Gladys!' she said.

'Same to you,' said Gladys. Alison was changed. 'Not so silly,' thought Gladys. 'I like her better now, I like lots of people better—but most of all Mirabel!'

'Good-bye, everybody!' yelled the twins. 'Merry Christmas and Happy New Year when they come!'

Good-bye! Don't eat too much Christmas-pudding, Anna!'

'Good-bye Elsie! Happy hols.!'

'Good-bye, Bobby! Think out a few more tricks. I say, *do* you remember Mam'zelle's face when the plate jumped?'

'Good-bye, Hilary. See you next term. Nice to think you'll be our head-girl again!'

'Good-bye, everybody! Good-bye!'